Ache

MEN OF HIDDEN CREEK

ALISON HENDRICKS

Cover design by AngstyG.

Createspace Edition.

ISBN-13: 978-1723246777

ACHE

KYLE

*K*yle Harris stood outside of his new home holding a box that contained a good quarter of his worldly possessions.

Okay, maybe that was an exaggeration, but he'd rented the smallest truck the place had and still there'd been a ton of room for him to move around. There wasn't any need to play moving day Tetris. The few pieces of furniture and the boxes full of his crap all played nicely together, and it wouldn't take him long to unload everything at all. He could probably manage it before Brandon even showed up, but his brother had insisted on helping and Kyle relented.

He owed Brandon too much to do anything else.

The front door was already propped open, and Kyle took the medium-sized box inside. His shoes made a soft thud on the carpeted floor as he walked through the entryway, past the very empty space that was to be his living room, and to the even emptier space that was his new bedroom. Whoever had lived here last had taken the window coverings with them, so the bright

Texas sun shone through the glass, casting rectangular shafts of light down on the floor. This room was going to bake in the summer afternoons, but the vents from the central AC would help.

He set the box down in the corner and withdrew his keys from his pocket, tearing through the packing tape in one sure swipe. The box was mostly filled with scrubs in various colors and patterns, along with two pairs of comfortable—and very stylish, in Kyle's opinion—sneakers. A frame rested in the bottom, wrapped in newspaper and celebrating his graduation from nursing school. There was another framed picture there, too, of Kyle with his and Brandon's dad on the day he'd graduated. His first ID badge and some other mementos rounded out the collection of items, the whole box describing a good portion of his life. The better portion of it, anyway. The portion that hadn't led him to Hidden Creek.

Kyle looked out the bare window, at the patchy stretch of green grass and the large trees that were still slightly bent to one direction from the hurricane. There was another house just beyond the fence, and more houses past that. It was a quiet, quaint neighborhood where people hung flags from their porches and grew flowers in their front yards. Maybe Kyle would see about growing something outside of this window. Maybe Katie might like to help him plant some bulbs.

He made his way back out to the driveway. One of his neighbors across the street was out mowing his lawn, and the man waved. Kyle waved back, offering a smile. After he signed the lease, he'd been greeted by a young couple who'd brought him a fresh apple pie as a housewarming gift. It sat on the counter now, waiting to be eaten. This was nothing like the city he'd come from. He'd lived in Dallas for almost ten years, and he couldn't have named any of his neighbors in the cramped apartment complex even if he'd been offered a million dollars to do so.

Things were different here, and Kyle desperately needed different.

As he ducked into the back of the truck, he heard tires on asphalt, the sound growing closer. When he stepped out to look, Brandon's white Chevy pulled into the driveway.

His older brother stood only a few inches taller than Kyle's five foot seven. His shaggy hair was a darker shade of blond, his trimmed goatee even darker. It was a face Kyle knew well, and at the same time, one he didn't know at all. The last time he'd seen Brandon was at their father's funeral, back when his brother had been a newlywed and his wife was four months pregnant.

"Hey," Brandon said, in that short way that made people unfamiliar with him think he was in a bad mood. "Sorry I'm late. Had to get Katie from school."

"It's no problem at all, man," Kyle said, "family comes first."

An awkward pause hung in the air, and Kyle desperately wished he hadn't said that. He and Brandon might have been half-brothers, but they were still brothers. They were still family. Even if Kyle hadn't acted like it for a long time.

The passenger door closed, and Brandon's daughter stepped around the front of the truck. She had platinum curls that would soon darken, if her father's genes had any say in it, and she looked up at Kyle with a shy smile. Determined not to screw up two interactions in one day, Kyle smiled back.

"You must be Katie. I'm your uncle Kyle." Could he claim that title as anything more than biology? "I'm... looking forward to getting to know you."

Because that was exactly what a ten-year-old cared about. Getting to know a complete stranger.

Katie just beamed at him, though, her smile full of rainbows and sunshine. It was so contagious that Kyle's gloomy mood lifted just a little. "Dad said I could help. If it's okay with you?"

"Yeah, of course," Kyle said, taken aback. She talked like she was sixteen, at least. And what ten-year-old wanted to help someone unpack? He looked up at his brother, and Brandon just shrugged. "Follow me."

He led her over to the U-Haul trailer and walked behind her as she made her way up the ramp, just in case she stumbled. Why she would, Kyle didn't know, but some weird, protective instinct kicked in and made him disregard the fact that Katie's mom was an award-winning gymnast. He pointed out another light box that was mostly filled with clothes, and the ten-year-old picked it up without complaint and started carrying it toward the open door.

Kyle just stared after her in amazement.

"She's a good kid," Brandon said, stepping into the truck. "No thanks to me."

"Somehow I doubt that." Because Brandon's ex traveled all the time, he had primary custody of Katie. At least, that was what Kyle remembered hearing.

Brandon just shrugged and looked around the half-empty trailer. "Did you sell a bunch of stuff before you left Dallas?"

Kyle let out a single note of dry laughter. "Rebecca."

His brother lifted his hands in the universal "say no more" gesture, and the two of them decided to bring in the couch first. They alternated with Katie, bringing in another piece of furniture while she carried in a box, and the whole truck was

4

unpacked in less than an hour. After that, the three of them stood awkwardly in Kyle's newly-furnished living room. There wasn't much to look at. Just a couch, a newly-mounted flat screen, a shelving unit, and one end table he'd picked up at Goodwill before he left Dallas. The absence of anything homey made the silence feel like a gaping vacuum, and Kyle finally had to break it.

"I don't know if you guys have time to stick around, but I was going to order a pizza or something." He paused, realizing he hadn't thought this through. "Um, there is a pizza place here that delivers, right?"

Brandon offered him a patient smile. "They have awesome pizza at Rocket. They should come out this far." He turned to his daughter. "How do you feel about pizza with Uncle Kyle, Katydid?"

"Can we get pineapple?" she asked, drawing her bottom lip between her teeth.

Wars had been started over the issue of whether pineapple was an appropriate topping for pizza, and when Brandon's gaze swung back his way, Kyle knew he was going to have to pick a side once and for all.

"How about it, Kyle? Are you a pineapple on your pizza kind of guy, or are you somebody who's wrong?" Brandon asked with a smirk that made his daughter giggle.

"Pineapple's fine with me. Maybe with some ham? Is that acceptable to the committee?"

Brandon looked at his daughter with a raised brow, and when she gave a thumbs up, he mirrored it. Laughing, Kyle pulled out his phone and made the order for a large Hawaiian pizza and a two-liter bottle of soda, since he suddenly realized he didn't have a damn thing in his fridge and he wasn't sure how the tap water tasted in Hidden Creek. Dallas' tap water had always had a chemical aftertaste to it that made it undrinkable without a filter.

As they waited for the pizza, Kyle hooked up his Nintendo Switch for his niece, feeling awful that he had no source of entertainment. She was instantly enamored, though, and it gave him the chance to pull Brandon into the kitchen and say what he'd spent ten years trying to sort out.

"I'm sorry I haven't been around for you. Or for her." He swallowed, watching as his brother cut open the tape on a box and started putting appliances on the counter. "After Dad died…"

"Don't worry about it, Ky." Ky. He hadn't been called that by anyone in ages. His heart clenched at the memory of weekends spent playing with his brother, wishing they had more time together. "You're here now. That's what matters."

There was a tension in Brandon's voice that offered more than his words alone did, and Kyle decided now definitely wasn't the time to talk about the man whose genes they'd shared. He was prepared to change the subject, but Brandon beat him to the punch.

"So… what happened with Rebecca, exactly? Aunt Shirley said you were happy."

Of course she had. Aunt Shirley was like a nexus in their family. Observations went in and gossip came out, spread far and wide over phone lines and internet cables. In this case, though, she'd been right.

"We were happy. Right up until the day before the wedding, when I caught her fucking my best friend." The word tasted bitter in his mouth, and Kyle made a face before amending, "Ex best friend."

Brandon winced, then offered a tentative hand on Kyle's shoulder. When Kyle didn't flinch or otherwise react negatively, he gave the man a squeeze. "Ouch. Here I thought my marriage had issues. At least Rebecca was never unfaithful. Not with a person, anyway. She just... loves her career more than me and Katie."

The last was said the way someone might describe an unfortunate accident. Oops, I forgot to close the door to the fridge. Oops, my wife is halfway across the country and sees her daughter maybe three times a year, if that. At least according to Aunt Shirley.

"Hey, it's not a contest," Kyle told him. "And if it is, it's a really terrible one."

Brandon flashed him a grin and patted his shoulder one last time before withdrawing his hand. He leaned back against the counter, and Kyle did the same at almost the same moment on the opposite side of the kitchen.

"Hidden Creek's a nice place. I think it'll be a good change for you. And whenever you're ready to start dating again, there's lots of opportunities for that, too."

He'd heard—again from Aunt Shirley—that there were way more single gay men in town than single women, which was just fine by Kyle. He wasn't interested in dating any time soon. From the moment he met her, he'd thought Rebecca was it for him. He was done. He'd found the love of his life. But apparently he wasn't hers, and that wasn't something he could easily recover from.

"Change is exactly what I need. New home, new job, new life," he mused. If he was going to have to reinvent himself after Rebecca, he was going to do it right.

"Then why don't you come out with me tonight?" Kyle opened his mouth to protest—Brandon had already done too much for him— but his brother kept on. "My neighbor can watch Katie for a couple hours, and it'll give us a chance to catch up."

He'd never been much of a drinker, and there was the little

problem of starting a twelve-hour shift first thing tomorrow morning. The last thing he needed to do was show up with a hangover. But he'd denied Brandon the chance to bond with him for long enough, and who knew? Maybe someone would catch his eye and he'd change that whole "no dating" policy. Hell, maybe he'd even go home with someone.

Change was the order of the day, and with change came risk. Kyle was ready for it all. So long as it took his mind off the mess that was his life, he'd throw himself at just about anything.

"You know what? A night out sounds perfect."

2

WES

*W*es sat at a quiet table in the corner of Bottom's Up, Hidden Creek's most popular gay bar, and watched the world pass by.

Couples filtered in through the night. Older, more established couples left by nine or ten, just stopping in to join co-workers or friends and let off some steam. Younger couples arrived later and stayed later, too, sometimes until last call. They had more to prove, to each other and to the world. And, to be completely fair, there wasn't a ton to do in Hidden Creek after hours.

Wes had always been a man who made his own fun, though. He'd learned to do it from a lifetime of living in this small town, and lately, a revolving door of men looking for a night they wouldn't soon forget but wouldn't be pressed to remember, either. Tonight he couldn't say he was in the mood to steal some fresh-faced young man away to the bathroom and give him a taste of what was to come if he decided to take a chance. Tonight he just wanted to drink and stew and forget that the whole day had ever happened.

He'd lost a patient.

It wasn't the first time, and it wouldn't be the last. He wasn't fucking infallible, as much as some people might think he was. Some of the staff whispered about the streak he'd maintained for nearly a month. Twenty-eight days, not a single death on his shift. But it wasn't something to brag about. In a small town like Hidden Creek, it should be the bare minimum, and if he lost anyone, it should be someone who was beyond help. Someone who'd lived a full life and was ready to meet their maker.

Not a nineteen-year-old boy who'd barely had enough time to experience anything.

He'd arrived in respiratory distress, and Wes had done everything in his power to clear the boy's airway and get his lungs to work properly. It hadn't helped. The patient stopped breathing completely and went into respiratory arrest. He lost consciousness from the lack of oxygen, then later went into cardiac arrest. A trifecta of shit hitting the fan. Wes had tried to revive him long past the time when the rest of his staff had called it, but it was no use.

Toxicology reports showed a high amount of opioids in his system, along with a high blood alcohol level. Senseless? Absolutely. Intentional? He had no idea. All Wes knew was that he'd ordered a pair of nurses out of the room after they'd commented on how awful it was; how something like this should have never happened in Hidden Creek. But it had been happening in so many rural areas that Wes knew it was only a matter of time before it struck here, and anyone who thought differently was delusional.

He lifted a single malt glass of Lagavulin Scotch to his lips and drank slowly. Smooth, fiery liquid slid down his throat with a burn that hurt so damn good every time. Tomorrow was another day. Tomorrow, he'd make sure every member of Hidden Creek

Memorial's staff knew the score when it came to overdoses and things that would "never happen" in their town. But tonight, he was going to drink his whiskey, and he was going to wallow.

It wasn't like Trevor Malhoney was the first patient he'd ever lost from completely preventable causes. It wasn't the worst, either, though Wes was reluctant to rank the loss of life. But in terms of deaths that personally affected him and shattered his life into millions of tiny, irreparable pieces? That honor went to someone else.

He took another long drink and stared out at the bar's patrons with a disinterested sweep. There were plenty of singles at Bottom's Up, intermixed and sometimes intermingling with the couples. Wes had a keen eye for spotting single men who were desperate for a satisfying fuck—and nothing else. Men who wanted to raise the stakes; do something out of their comfort zone. That was his type when it came to one-night stands. Men who would feel slightly ashamed of how wantonly they'd acted the night before, but not enough to try and deny that it ever happened.

Normally, Wes would have searched out exactly that kind of entertainment for his evening, but Bottom's Up was crowded mostly with locals tonight, and he wasn't interested in turning any of his one-night stands into two-night stands—despite the lust-filled looks he was getting from a couple of men dressed in too-tight jeans.

Other than a cursory stirring as his cock recognized a good fuck, they didn't do anything for him tonight. He was "too far up his own ass," as Adrian was fond of saying.

Wes' heart squeezed painfully at the memory, and he drowned out the feeling by finishing his glass and ordering another round. As he waited, he pulled out his phone and thumbed through his social media accounts, noticing a Grindr message from Swishy Like Wine that he promptly ignored. He scrolled past tweet after tweet, post after post, nothing catching his interest.

As his mind wandered, though, he heard something far more captivating than anything his so-called friend circle could manage.

"We stopped sleeping together a little bit after the engagement." A young man—late twenties at the most—spoke to someone slightly older with similar features. A brother? "She told me she wanted it to feel new again." An intoxicated snort followed this. "Such a load of bullshit. She just wanted to fuck Mike without a guilty conscience."

Interesting. He might as well have been left at the altar. Wes was willing to bet anything that this Mike was a friend, too. It fit the narrative too well for him to be some stranger.

"Man. What'd you do when you caught them? I mean, were they—"

"Fucking right in front of me?" the first man offered. From the bitter look on his face, Wes knew the answer. "Yep. I got a good look at Mike's hairy ass as he plowed my fiancée. Great stuff."

The younger of the two tossed back a drink and Wes took that moment to admire his form. The alcohol kissed lips that looked soft and pliant. Just thick enough to suck on with some satisfaction. The strong muscles in his throat worked as he swallowed, and Wes imagined the man on his knees and swallowing something else entirely. His dick twitched in his dark pants, and he let his gaze drag slowly over the rest of the man's body.

He had a lean build, fit but not the type that frequented the gym. His job must have involved some kind of exercise, or he was a runner. Lithe limbs and a tapered body supported that idea, and when the man shifted a certain way on his stool, Wes got a tantalizing look at his tight ass, cruelly confined in a pair of jeans. A rumble caught in his throat, and he very nearly had to adjust himself under the cover of the table as he thought of all the things he'd like to do to that body.

Wes could slip away with him to the bathroom, lock the door and shove the slender man up against it, so that luscious ass stuck out to greet him. He could slip his arms around the stranger, one hand sliding under his shirt, the other moving down to grip his dick through his pants while he ground his own leaking cock against the man's ass. He could turn him around, ease him down to the floor and unzip his fly before feeding his cock to his partner's wet, waiting mouth...

He nearly groaned as the fantasy played itself out in his mind, and this time he did have to shift in his chair to ease the painful erection somewhat. This little lost pup of a man had given no indication of being interested in men, but Wes was eager to find out, and he'd made more than one supposedly straight boy realize they were incredibly bi. Opening up a whole new world to them was like performing a public service, and he would be oh so happy to service that man.

The dreary mood he'd come into Bottom's Up with slipped away, and Wes found himself fixated on the out-of-towner and biding his time until the man was alone.

3

KYLE

The hairs on the back of Kyle's neck stood on end as he suddenly felt eyes on him.

He was telling Brandon the details of his not-so-amicable split with Rebecca and his best man, Mike, his hands flying in wild gestures the deeper he got into it.

He wasn't drunk. Not yet, anyway. A couple of beers did not a drunk Harris make, but he could admit if he were to leave the comfort of his stool, he might stumble just a little bit. And he definitely wasn't feeling as reserved as he might under normal circumstances.

Maybe that was why he noticed he'd caught someone's attention. He hadn't really expected it, considering Brandon had taken them to a gay bar. He'd always suspected his brother was bi, but in this instance, he'd just explained that Bottom's Up had a more inviting atmosphere, and Kyle had definitely felt the effects of that. When there was a break in the conversation—when Brandon's phone rang and he went to take the call outside—he finally ventured a glance at his admirer.

When he did, he found a tall man in his mid to late thirties with a penetrating steel-gray stare and thick black hair that almost shone with touches of blue in the neon lights. A wide mouth was tipped up in a smirk that exuded confidence, and Kyle felt a shiver run up his spine as the man's gaze roved shamelessly over his body.

He was being checked out by another man. No, not just checked out. Practically eye-fucked, if the heat in the stranger's gaze was anything to go off of.

Aunt Shirley had a field day with all the gossip she was able to scoop up from the amount of single gay men in Hidden Creek, but somehow Kyle hadn't expected he'd ever end up on anyone's radar. He was average. Ordinary. The kind of man who could lose himself in a crowd, leaving no one the wiser.

The fact that he'd caught the attention of someone like that was flattering, to say the least. Kyle had no problem admitting another man was attractive. Hot, even. Smoking hot, like some untouchable actor or superstar athlete.

The man knew it, too. He leaned back in his booth, arms spread wide over the back of it to reveal broad shoulders and a muscular chest hugged tight by his button-down shirt.

Kyle should have felt a little uncomfortable with the deliberate looks he was getting; looks that lingered on even when he turned away. But a strange thrill coursed through his body, adrenaline pumping through his veins, a flush overtaking his skin. The signs of attraction if he'd ever felt them.

Strange, because he'd never been attracted to another man before. But maybe there were some people who just transcended the lines of sexuality. His best friend in nursing school was straight as an arrow, or so she said, but she also said she'd happily be Olivia Wilde's sex slave if the offer ever arose. There was also the fact that every straight man he knew seemed to be obsessed with Chris Evans.

The thought was cut short as Brandon returned, phone still in hand. He held it up with an apologetic look on his face.

"That was my neighbor. Apparently Katie had a bad dream, and she was upset I wasn't there…"

Kyle waved him off. "Say no more. Go take care of your daughter, Bran. We've got plenty of time to catch up."

"I hope so," Brandon said with a tentative smile before he grabbed his coat. "If you stay, feel free to keep it on my tab, okay? Kris knows I'm good for it."

"I'll probably just finish off this beer and head home," Kyle admitted, though there was a tingle deep down that told him he might have other opportunities. "I start at the hospital tomorrow, seven sharp."

Brandon grimaced, patting his brother on the back. "Go easy on the drinks, then. Getting up that early's bad enough."

Kyle would have said the same thing years ago, but he'd gotten used to it. Twelve-hour shifts flashed in the blink of an eye when the clinic was busy, and he hoped it would be the same at the hospital.

As soon as Brandon left, he felt that intense stare focus on him again.

His body heated rapidly, like he was standing too close to a raging inferno. His cock was even starting to respond, proving his point about some peoples' ability to be attractive to both genders.

When he stole another glance at the booth, he saw it suddenly empty. An odd sense of disappointment flooded him, but it was replaced by the thundering of his pulse as he realized the man was heading right for him.

"Evening."

His voice was smooth, touched with only the hint of a Texan accent. Kyle imagined he was like one of those men in the old movies who sat in the parlor and enjoyed a nice glass of whiskey while smoking a cigar. That was what he sounded like, at least, and that one word sent another shiver racing through him.

Jesus Christ. What was going on?

"Evening," Kyle said, offering the man a friendly smile as he turned to face him.

The man was standing close. Very close. He leaned casually against the bar, one arm resting against it. Kyle could smell his cologne, some spicy mixture with undertones that smelled like the forest. And something else, too. Maybe whoever made that cologne had injected liquid pheromones into it, because the man before him exuded dominance, and Kyle felt like a helpless rabbit caught in a hunter's snare.

"Wes Monroe," he said, offering a hand. "I couldn't help but over-hear you talking to your... brother? Unless you've just got a thing for guys who look a little like you."

He flashed Kyle a grin, displaying two rows of perfectly straight teeth the way a predator might display his fangs. His heart thumped dangerously behind his rib cage, and it was enough to make him fight back with the only tool he had at his disposal: Snark.

"Couldn't help, or listened in like a creep?"

Wes' grin only broadened. Apparently he liked his prey showing a bit of backbone. Kyle swallowed, his Adam's apple bobbing as he did so, and looked down at the man's still outstretched hand.

"You're a loud drunk," he pointed out, continuing before Kyle could protest, "but I was listening in. Couldn't be helped when you're the most interesting thing in this bar."

The man's gaze took a shameless journey over the planes of Kyle's body, and he swore he could feel those large hands undressing him, smoothing over his bare skin, moving down and down until—

"It's awful rude not to shake a man's hand when he offers."

Kyle snorted at that. "And staring at somebody like you want to devour them isn't?"

Wes' eyes flashed, but that grin remained in place, and his hand stayed outstretched, waiting for something he knew he'd get. A moment later, Kyle reached out to take it.

Flesh pressed to flesh, and it was as if Wes had pulled him in chest to chest. Heat radiated from their palms, and Wes' grip around his hand was firm, confident, almost possessive, as he gave one firm pump.

Kyle's mind conjured an image of that big hand wrapped around his dick, pumping him expertly, aggressively, until he came. It was enough to steal the breath from his lungs and he searched to find his voice.

"Kyle," he finally introduced himself, clearing his throat. "And yeah, Brandon's my brother. He lives out here—"

"On Sycamore, with his daughter. Katie, right?" At the look Kyle shot him, Wes continued after a laugh. "It's a small town. Everybody knows everybody here."

Wes didn't bother letting go of his hand, Kyle realized, and he'd started tracing tight circles against the underside of his wrist that mesmerized Kyle.

"So. Kyle. You here visiting, or is this a more permanent thing?"

He managed to pull himself away from the rhythmic motion only to become caught in Wes' intense grey eyes.

"Just moved here," he answered, swallowing. "If you 'accidentally overheard' my conversation with Brandon, you know why."

"I'm sorry she hurt you," Wes said, stepping just a hair closer. Enough that Kyle could feel the heat coming off of his body. "But I'm not sorry you ended up here. Just means I get to enjoy you instead."

Blood pounded in Kyle's ears, nearly drowning out the sexually-charged words. There was no mistaking the intent. Wes wasn't even trying to be subtle.

Now was the time when he should tell the man he wasn't interested; that he wasn't into men that way. But that seemed like a blatant lie, considering his cock was currently pressing hard against the seam of his pants—something he was sure Wes noticed.

Some part of him was attracted to this man. Some part of him wanted this man. Wanted those wide, smirking lips, that big, broad body, those strong, teasing hands. Some part of him wanted it so bad that a tremor rocked through him, making his knees buckle.

"You sound awfully confident for a man who just met me," Kyle murmured, the rest of the bar disappearing as he looked up at Wes.

The corner of those gorgeous lips tipped up even further. "I'm a confident man."

"Or an arrogant one."

"Six of one, half dozen of the other..." The circles Wes was making with his thumb grew wider, venturing further up his arm.

Kyle licked his suddenly dry lips, looking up at the taller man. "I'm not looking for anything."

"Neither am I," Wes confirmed, stepping that much closer. He was inches away now, and Kyle swore he could almost hear the man's racing heartbeat. "Just you. In my bed."

Fuck. He'd never been on the other end of this exchange. Hell, he'd never been part of this exchange, period. He didn't have this man's confidence, this certainty that he was wanted. It was as irritating as it was sexy, and Kyle wanted to turn him down flat as much as he wanted to find the nearest private space and get pressed up against the wall by this man.

He was straight. That was what he'd always thought, anyway. But apparently he just hadn't found the type of guy who did anything for him. Until tonight. His libido was firing on all cylinders now, lust running hot through his veins, and he was running out of reasons to say no.

You have to work tomorrow.

You'll see this man around town.

You're supposed to be bonding with your brother, not fucking a stranger.

You don't have the first clue about being with a man.

None of those arguments seemed to matter right now. For whatever reason, Wes wanted him, and he hadn't felt wanted in a long time. Longer than he'd been willing to admit to his brother. Proposing to Rebecca was his last-ditch effort to get her to act like she gave a damn about their relationship, but it hadn't worked. Even if it had... things had never been like this between them. If he threw a match down right now, he was positive it would catch fire and burn down to the stick before it ever hit the ground.

"We can draw this out. Get to know each other over a couple drinks—my treat." Wes' eyes burned like molten steel. "Or you can leave with me right now, and I can make you forget all about your ex."

God, that sounded good. That was why he was here, wasn't it? To make a change so drastic that he couldn't help but leave his old life behind him? And what better way to do that than exploring this newest facet of his sexuality with someone who didn't know the old Kyle?

"Yeah. Okay."

Two words. Two simple words, and he'd sealed his fate. Kyle's whole body felt like it was on fire as he stood, with Wes' assistance. The man made no attempt to hide the fact that he was caressing Kyle's arm in the process, and Kyle felt goosebumps raise all along his bicep.

"My place isn't far," Wes whispered, his lips almost brushing against the back of Kyle's neck.

He should text Brandon and let him know he was leaving the bar, but right now all he could think about was getting out of the public eye. Wes gestured, and Kyle led him out the door of the bar. If anyone had noticed their sexually-charged encounter, they were nice enough to ignore it, as a quick glance around Bottom's Up revealed no one watching them.

He walked out into the chilly night, blasted by the cold as soon as he set foot outside. It hadn't been this cold in Dallas. There were lots of buildings around to block the breeze, and all the sidewalks and facades practically radiated heat once the sun had dipped below the horizon. He wasn't complaining, though. The man who left behind him—and then quickly fell in stride with him—gave off enough heat to rival any of those buildings.

They walked in silence, no cars on the road, no people milling about. Anywhere else, it might have felt eerie, but here it was peaceful. In the distance he saw the lights of a diner that was still open, and he slipped his hands into his pockets, just enjoying the view while his nerves coiled tighter and tighter in anticipation. Wes stopped suddenly at a curb, and Kyle's immediate instinct was to look for traffic. There was none, and the one stoplight in sight flashed yellow.

He turned to find his companion looking at him with a mix of lust and a sobering amount of seriousness.

"My apartment's just up there," he said, nodding to a nearby apartment building. "We can part ways here, no hard feelings. Or..."

Had he sensed Kyle's hesitation? The thought made him anxious, but that was nothing to the sudden hit of almost desperate lust that slammed into him. This man had awoken something he didn't know was inside of him, and Kyle's body was eager to experience everything he had to offer—even if his brain was rationally aware of the fact that he was stumbling into this blind.

"Do you need me to write it in a letter? Engrave it on a plaque? Etch it into stone? Burn it—"

He wasn't able to finish the snarky remark or think about why he apparently copped one hell of an attitude when he was nervous. Wes' mouth came crashing down on his, and his big body forced him back against the nearest wall. His lips were softer than Kyle expected, even if the kiss was hard and unrelenting. Wes' stubble scraped his face as Kyle kissed him back with equal hunger, his arms going over the man's broad shoulders, fingers gripping tight.

Wes thrust his tongue into Kyle's mouth, drawing a moan from the man and making him feel like the most shameless of horny teenagers as he arched against his partner, trying desperately for some friction that would soothe his aching dick. Wes took charge, his hands gripping Kyle's hips as he ground their bodies together, seam to seam, their cocks separated by thin layers of fabric.

Kyle's head fell back against the wall and he let out a loud moan. So loud that Wes clapped his hand over the man's mouth and whispered in his ear. "Save that for later. You can be as loud as you want once I close the door."

He pulled away after that and composed himself like they hadn't just been making out and grinding against each other in the middle of town. Kyle was panting, his eyes wide as he watched the ease with which Wes recovered—all but his cock, which still tented a large bulge in his pants. He was used to this, obviously, but Kyle definitely wasn't. He'd just kissed another man, and while it was different from anything he'd experienced before, it was exactly what he needed at that moment.

Even still, his mouth hung open as Wes just smirked, turned, and started toward the apartment building. Then he followed, caught up in a spell that seemed impossible to break.

4

WES

*W*es managed to restrain himself on the elevator ride up to his apartment. While he didn't mind the prospect of being caught on camera—the security guard on duty was free to stroke one out at his leisure—there was something to be said for keeping a partner in suspense. He'd all but mauled Kyle on the way there, and one glance at the man was enough to tell Wes he expected similar treatment as they slowly ascended the floors. But Wes just smiled, stuffed his hands into his pockets, and acted like he wasn't tenting the fabric with his very painful erection.

He didn't say a word, even when the doors parted on his floor. He simply stepped out and strode toward his apartment, fishing out his keys at the last moment. Despite the touch of "I've never done this before" nervousness, Wes could feel the anticipation rolling off Kyle in waves—the man was practically vibrating with it. He was wound as tightly as he could be, and Wes' lips curved as he thought of just how fun it would be to finally snap him.

He stepped inside first, waiting for Kyle to cross the threshold and close the door behind them. The instant it shut, Wes' calm, confident demeanor suddenly flared into pure hunger. His hands gripped Kyle's wrists and he pinned the man back against the door, the length of his body covering Kyle's. Hard lines met in heated motion, Wes' lips claiming his in a bruising kiss. Kyle moaned against him, the sound of a man who was utterly lost and just dying for someone to show him the way.

His tongue thrust into Kyle's wet, eager mouth, tasting the hint of alcohol and some other sweet flavor that seemed unique to the man. It would have been easy for Kyle to let him take control; to surrender and just let Wes do everything in his power to make them both feel good, but Kyle had more agency, more fight in him than that. His arms flexed under Wes' grip, and when he realized he wasn't going to get free on his own, he lifted his ass away from the door, his hips meeting Wes' in a desperate bid.

Wes growled, biting down on Kyle's lower lip just enough to let him know he was in charge. But Kyle didn't submit. Like a smaller wolf challenging the alpha, he pushed back, grinding his hard cock against Wes', driving him to distraction with that simple motion.

Afraid he might just give in and fuck the man only a few steps into his apartment—even if that wasn't an undesirable outcome—Wes pulled back. His lips tipped into a smirk as he looked at the half-lidded Kyle before slowly releasing his hands, and then turning to walk deeper into the apartment as though nothing had happened.

"Drink?" he asked nonchalantly, moving to the kitchen.

Kyle was very obviously dazed, but he shook off the feeling in record time—enough to make a substantial quip. "You're kind of an asshole, aren't you?"

Wes wore an amused smile, but he kept his back to Kyle as he poured them both two fingers of whiskey each. Crossing the room, he handed one glass to Kyle and raised the other to his lips with a devilish smile. "I'm hurt that you underestimate me. I'm every bit an asshole, and if you didn't like it, you wouldn't be here."

Kyle considered that a moment, then just shrugged as if accepting his fate. Wes nodded toward the couch, and the two of them took a more comfortable position. As comfortable as could be managed when Wes constantly had to adjust himself.

"This place is a lot fancier than anywhere else I've seen in Hidden Creek. Don't tell me you're some corporate CEO?"

Wes let out a low sound of amusement, then took a sip of whiskey. The smooth amber liquid burned all the way down his throat, and his eyes closed as he appreciated the sensation. "Much more important than that. I save lives."

Most of the time, at least. Wes knew he was a difficult man to work with, but he made up for it by having one of the best save rates in Texas. Considering Hidden Creek had limited resources, he'd always prided himself on his ability to quickly read a situation and make split second decisions. But even he wasn't infallible, and Adrian's gentle face kept playing through his mind. Beautiful and full of life one moment, ashen and still the next.

He swallowed down another sip and forced the thoughts from his mind, steel grey eyes focusing on the man who sat beside him, seeming amused by his arrogance. Wes' first thought was that he enjoyed that bratty little smirk, but he'd also like to find some way to alter it. A kiss would do the trick easily enough, though there were far more interesting ways to go about it. Ways that would make that smirk a distant memory as Kyle's lips parted and his eyes rolled back.

His gaze trailed down the man's body, imagining the warm skin that lay beneath. Would he have chest hair? A perfectly formed trail that started just below his navel and pointed the way to his cock? Just looking at the bulge in the man's pants, Wes could tell he was a decent size. Not unwieldy, but large enough to give his mouth something to do.

Would he be cut or uncut? Thick in girth, or more on the long side? Wes' mouth practically started to water as he imagined the intoxicating scent of sweat and musk, and the salty taste of another man's precum as he teased mercilessly. He'd take just the head of Kyle's cock into his mouth, run his tongue over the slit and beneath the crown, sucking lightly until Kyle begged him for more. The man might try to demand it, his hips rising off the couch, but Wes would hold him down if he had to, exploring as he desired, and only giving in when Kyle was a writhing mass of pure need.

"Something you want to share?" Kyle asked, interrupting his thoughts. That smirk was still in place, and it only grew at catching Wes daydreaming.

But he was hardly going to apologize. Nor would he play coy. Kyle had asked, and he'd get a solid answer.

"I'd rather show than tell, but since you asked, I was thinking about working your dick with my mouth until you beg me to stop."

He looked right at Kyle, right into the man's eyes as he said it. To his surprise, Kyle's pale skin flushed a lovely shade of pink, and that smirk was swept away by an obvious expression of want. Determined to forget about the day's failures, Wes took that as enthusiastic consent. He took one last sip of whiskey then set the glass aside before reaching for Kyle's. The younger man just watched, transfixed. Fingers brushed, an electric spark arced through the air, and Wes had to compose himself as he set the other glass aside.

Leaning over the couch, he moved one hand behind Kyle's head, his fingers sliding through thick, messy hair and curling tight as he brought the man closer. Whiskey was fresh on lips and tongues, a delicious burn that only added to the kiss as their mouths met. Kyle kissed with the fervor and energy of a man who'd been rejected far too many times, but who wasn't willing to simply cower and accept second best.

And Wes would reward him for that, to the point where he'd forget all about his ex-fiancée, at least for a night. It wasn't a long-term solution. Wes had never been very good at those. But it would give them both the distraction they were looking for, and they could figure out tomorrow when the sun's early morning rays slipped through his window.

Moving his free hand down Kyle's chest, he followed the planes and lines like they were a roadmap, all of them drawing down toward his real goal. He'd take the time to explore later and develop a better appreciation for the entirety of his partner's form, but those fantasies had stoked a fire in him, and he needed to feel the other man's cock pulsing greedily in his hand.

So his hand didn't stop at the waistband of Kyle's pants. He searched out the belt buckle and undid it, a thrill shooting through him at the sound of the metal clinking. Long, dexterous fingers—a surgeon's fingers, one of his professors had told him—fiddled with the buttons, pushing them through the holes before he went to the man's zipper.

Either Kyle hadn't noticed yet, or he wasn't bothered by it. His focus was still on the kiss; on trying to win a battle of wills that Wes would never let him—or anyone else—win. He'd only ever let one man dictate the terms of his sex life, and while he'd found a certain kind of enjoyment in it, the circumstances were far different from any casual fling.

He'd loved Adrian and he would've done anything to please him.

Kyle was a stranger, though. A newcomer to town who was at his mercy. Wes would show him the time of his life, make him come at least two or three times, and then they'd part ways. They'd see each other again. It was inevitable in Hidden Creek. But with any luck, the encounter would be a one-time thing. Best remembered at the peak of enjoyment, not the misery that came from a long-term engagement.

He gripped the zipper between two fingers, sliding it down just enough to get his hand into Kyle's pants. Soft, silky fabric greeted him, and he pressed on, looking for the opening. A small snap was undone, and Wes' palm rested over the ridge of Kyle's erection, his fingers curling as he gripped him through the fabric.

His partner gasped into his mouth, which Wes took as a sure sign of his pleasure. But then Kyle drew back, and his hand shot down to grab Wes' wrist.

"Wait," he said, breathless.

Wes stopped immediately, his fingers uncurling, Kyle's cock woefully untouched even though he could still feel the molten heat emanating from the man. His eyes met Kyle's mossy green ones, and it was easy to see the man was nervous; uncertain.

"I've... never done this before," he admitted, blowing out a breath. "With another man, I mean."

That had been easy enough to guess from Kyle's surprised reaction to him. There wasn't any need to point it out and bruise the poor boy's ego, though. Instead, Wes just leaned further over him and murmured, "I'm a fantastic teacher."

In the bedroom, at least. Medical students locked themselves in their cars and cried after spending the day with him. Or so he'd been told.

He claimed Kyle's mouth in another hungry kiss, his hand staying where it was until he felt the man relax, even if his thighs were still insanely tense. Wes massaged gently, then moved inward again, more than ready to reveal his prize so he could at least get answers to some of his question.

But then Kyle pulled away, shifting in a way that better hid his arousal. Wes sat back and observed the man. He was blushing adorably, but there was something in his eyes that spoke of more than just inexperience. He wasn't ready for this step. Wes was moving too fast, this encounter was too casual, and Kyle hadn't had the chance to process what he wanted.

Ice water coursed through his veins, putting a sudden and painful end to his anticipation. He leaned back, returning to his cushion, and picked up the glass from the end table, offering it to Kyle. The younger man took it and drank gratefully.

"Sorry," he mumbled, seeming genuinely bothered by his reaction. "I wanted something different. I guess I'm just... not ready for that big of a change."

His eyes cast to Wes' sheepishly, and Wes set his own needs and desires aside long enough to offer an understanding smile. He knew what it was like to flail about helplessly, not knowing what exactly you wanted and what you were ready for. It'd happened in high school for him, years and years ago, but that didn't make Kyle's realization of his queerness any less substantial.

Yes, Wesley Monroe was an asshole of the highest order. He claimed that title with pride. But he wasn't the kind of guy who would force anyone into doing something—especially this. He'd never believed the "first time should be special" rhetoric, but it—and every time after—should be Kyle's choice, not just something he coerced himself into doing because of a bitter breakup.

"You don't have to apologize. No one should make you do something you aren't ready to do," Wes said simply. Kyle just stared at him, evidently convinced those words could not possibly have come out of his mouth. Wes' lips twitched into a smirk. "What? Do I really come across as that much of an asshole?"

"Would you blame me for saying yes?"

He laughed, some of that tension easing in him. It didn't hurt that he'd taken another sip of whiskey, too. "Not really."

"It's just, you seem like the kind of guy who does this all the time, and I'm... not. Not with women, not at all," Kyle admitted, curling up on his corner of the couch.

There was no need to ask what "this" was. Wes would happily admit he was the kind of guy who would take home a different man every night if Hidden Creek had that wide of a selection on offer. After the first time, there were only a couple years in his life where he'd stuck with one partner. All through med school and residency, he'd made the most of his limited free time by seducing any man who looked like he might be fun for a night.

"You're hurting. I get it," Wes said, setting his glass down. "If you're worried you've hurt my feelings or anything like that, don't be. I'm a big boy. I can take it."

He winked at that, and Kyle's attention was instantly drawn down to Wes' crotch. Though he wasn't aching as painfully anymore, he was still hard, and he shifted proudly, having not an ounce of shame. Kyle's cheeks burned.

"It's not for lack of wanting to. I've never really been attracted to men before, but tonight..."

"I'll take that as a compliment," Wes said.

"It is." There was a hunger in Kyle's voice, tinged with a sadness that said hunger wasn't going to be eased. Not tonight, anyway, and not with Wes. "I just need time to think. I mean, I'm in my mid-twenties." A little younger than Wes assumed. Interesting. "I never expected to start questioning my sexuality."

"There's no expiration date for queerness," Wes said with a smirk. "I realized I was gay when I was fourteen and having my hand on Becky Felton's tit did nothing for me." Kyle snorted at that. "I've met men who didn't realize it until they were in their thirties or forties. Some even later than that. Your life and your experiences are yours, Kyle. Live them the way you want. If that means finding someone to engage in awkward teenage pawing with you for a while until you're comfortable with more, then..." he lifted his glass as if in toast.

"Yeah, I don't think that's what it means." His tongue darted out, sweeping over his soft lips. If Wes didn't know better, he would have thought he was being taunted. "I just need some time to come to terms with it all, you know?"

"I do." Wes flashed him a grin. "I can't count how many porn clips I watched before I felt comfortable sucking a guy off."

Kyle had his glass up to his mouth, whiskey past his lips when he suddenly coughed and sputtered and turned beet red again. Wes could have lied and said he hadn't done that on purpose, but where was the fun in that?

"Is that your recommendation, then? Hours of gay porn?"

"More like days," Wes said without missing a beat.

Kyle laughed, a hearty, unashamed sound. It made him smile and seemed to work as just as much of a balm as fucking him would have. Seeing this man relaxed and enjoying himself—unafraid of being forced into something he wasn't ready for—it made Wes feel strangely warm. Almost like he was looking out for someone; passing along courtesies he'd never really been given.

"Do whatever works for you, though it is a relatively safe space to explore what turns you on," he finally said, his tone sobering. "And if we ever see each other again once you've figured things out…"

The rest of that statement hung in the air, a promise Wes hadn't intended to keep. There were other men out there, and no reason to wait around for Kyle to be at the same stage he was. But some part of him leapt at the challenge of showing the man what he'd been missing. So much so that he was sure he mirrored the heat in Kyle's eyes.

The younger man swallowed his whiskey heavily, then set the glass aside and stood. A playful smile tugged at Wes' lips as he realized something Kyle had forgotten.

"You may want to do something about that," he said, inclining his chin to indicate Kyle's undone belt and pants.

"Jesus," the man muttered, doing up zipper and buttons quickly, then fumbling with the belt. "That would've been awkward. Not really something I want to explain to my brother…"

Wes almost asked about Kyle's brother, who was inevitably the other man he'd seen at the bar. He almost asked about what Kyle was planning on doing now, if he had a job lined up, where he was living. Things he had no business asking someone who hadn't even been a one-night stand. Something about Kyle was painfully endearing, though, and that was why he needed to get the man out of his apartment.

"The Lyft driver would've told you," he transitioned smoothly, "do you want me to get someone?"

"No, thanks. Brandon was supposed to swing back by, which I forgot about when I followed you out of Bottom's Up…" Kyle ruffled a hand through his hair, his nerves seeming to grow by the moment. Wes just remained on the couch, lounging as non-threateningly as he could manage. "I'm gonna head out. Thanks for... well, not being as much of an asshole as you could've been."

"That's the sweetest thing anyone's ever said to me," Wes lobbed back.

Kyle laughed again, shook his head, and then let himself out of the apartment, leaving Wes alone with his thoughts—and his disappointments.

5

KYLE

*A*ll in all, after drinking way too much and making a complete ass of himself last night, Kyle felt all right.

Maybe it was because of the fact that Brandon hadn't dared ask him what he'd gotten up to. Maybe it was just lost in the trepidation and excitement he felt over his new job at Hidden Creek Memorial. The last thing he wanted to do was put his scrubs on inside out or forget the ID badge he'd been assigned after the job offer was made. Both seemed plausible if he hadn't managed to pull his shit together and focus on having an uneventful morning.

But as Kyle showered, all he could think about was Wes. He didn't even know the man's last name, he just knew that tower of lean muscle all wrapped up in a cocky facade made him feel things he'd never felt before. In the heat of the moment, he'd been ready to do just about anything for the man, so long as his mouth kept moving so expertly and his hand kept up its path to his aching dick.

He wasn't even sure he would've regretted it. Yes, it would've all happened in a blur, but Wes seemed like the kind of man who knew exactly what he was doing. He'd felt comfortable with the man, even safe, for all the predatory stares he'd gotten throughout the night. Those feelings were only amplified when Wes—who'd obviously just been looking for an easy hookup— had responded with kindness and compassion. He hadn't mocked Kyle for his lack of experience. He hadn't tried to cajole him into more. He hadn't made any promises he knew he wouldn't keep.

He'd just been supportive and understanding, much more than Kyle would have expected. So much so that he suspected there was a soft, gooey center to Wes' hard, sexy exterior.

He knew he'd see the man again. Hidden Creek was only so big, and there were only so many places to go out for a drink or get a bite to eat. Hell, he could already imagine seeing Wes at something as mundane as a gas station, filling up whatever fancy car he owned at the next pump over. Totally ordinary, and not something he needed to think about in the context of that same man having his hand on Kyle's cock.

Nope. Definitely not.

The sun had just barely started to scrape over the horizon, but Kyle was already wide awake and ready to start the day. He'd annoyed the Charge Nurse at his old hospital with his peppy morning person routine, but eventually she'd come to value the fact that Kyle could pick up everyone's morning rounds without missing a beat.

With any luck, he'd do the same at Hidden Creek Memorial. As he fixed his ID tag to his scrubs and checked himself in the mirror, Kyle vowed not to fantasize about Wes for the rest of the day. There'd be time to sort out his sexuality later.

"YOU TOLD HIM, RIGHT?" BETH WAS THE THIRD RN TO ASK THAT question of the current on-duty Charge Nurse, Vivian.

"First thing I said to him." Her pronounced Texan accent flowed like honey, making his own seem fake by comparison, as if he hadn't lived in Texas all his life.

"I haven't had time to make a Bingo sheet yet," Kyle joked, "but I'm pretty sure I just won."

Beth grinned at him. She was a short, stocky woman in her mid-thirties who—according to Vivian—went out of her way to make sure her patients got the best possible care. Even if that meant losing face with—or outright arguing with—the doctors. Kyle already knew the two of them were going to get along amazingly.

"I've dealt with difficult doctors before. I've made a whole career out of getting talked down to," he said with a smirk. "I can't say I'm that scared of Dr. Monroe."

Beth clicked her tongue behind her teeth, and Vivian made a low sound of disbelief, shaking her head. "Your funeral," she added in a sing-song tone.

"She tell you about the time Monroe made Annie cry in front of her patient?"

"Yep," Kyle confirmed. "She asked for clarification on his Diazepam order and he snapped. Seen it before. Doctors think they're beyond reproach."

It was one thing he'd always known to be true. In an ideal hospital settings, nurses and doctors would work together to provide the best patient care possible. But more often than not, doctors brought a superiority complex to the job. They always took it poorly when a nurse—someone who, to them, had to endure a lot less suffering for their position—questioned anything they did, from med orders to discharge write-ups.

Kyle, of course, had never given a damn. He'd grown up the youngest of four children, all boys. He was used to people treating him like a second-rate citizen. As much as he loved his brothers, they were complete assholes when it came to him being a nurse. He'd learned to ignore it a long time ago, from pretty much the moment he decided on nursing as a career path.

And if he didn't let his own family push him around, he definitely wasn't going to let some hotshot doctor do it. The guy was probably ancient; part of the old guard. The type of person who used social terms and labels that had fallen out of favor twenty or thirty years ago.

"I'm not worried," he said, offering Beth and Vivian a friendly smile. "So long as he doesn't treat the patients that way, we won't have a problem."

"Oh he's the perfect gentleman to every patient who walks through that door," Vivian said, rolling her eyes. "Calm, kind, attentive. He'll sit there and answer questions for an hour while somebody rattles off all the things they read on the internet about their diagnosis."

Nice to patients but not nurses? Interesting. Either he really did consider himself above people like Kyle, or he had some kind of outstanding beef.

Beth had another theory. "He does that just to spite us, you know, so we look like the unreasonable ones if we ever complain to Sloane." Her voice deepened, imitating the director Kyle had met during his interview. "His patient satisfaction rating is impeccable, Bethany. Have you considered the idea that maybe Dr. Monroe isn't the common problem here?"

Vivian groaned. "Did he honestly say that to you?"

The conversation changed to griping about Sloane, and while

Kyle definitely wanted to endear himself to his co-workers, trash-talking everybody's boss on day one seemed like a bad idea. So the instant there was a break in the conversation, he took the opportunity to do something useful.

"It looked like there was a patient in three when I came in," he noted, "have they been seen yet?"

"Mmhmm," Vivian said, navigating the patient files on an ancient CRT hooked up to an only slightly less ancient PC. She smacked the hard case of the monitor after several long moments of silence. "Damn thing's locked up again. I swear we'd get a lot more patients in and out of here if they'd actually spring for some computers that were made after 1999."

Kyle visibly winced, hoping that was an exaggeration. Considering the monitor, he doubted it.

"Three's a migraine," Beth said. "Dr. Monroe's supposed to see her whenever he bothers to drag his ass into work."

"Do you mind if I follow up? I want the patients to know who I am, so they can grab me if they need me."

Plus it would give him a chance to get the initial meeting with Dr. Monroe over with as soon as possible. After that, he could just go on to having a productive day.

"Be my guest," Vivian said. "If you take any vitals, just mark 'em in her chart. I recommend getting in and out quickly though, if you don't want to bump into His Royal Highness."

Kyle let out a soft snort of amusement. "I'll keep that in mind," he said as he turned to head off to curtain three.

It wasn't nearly as much of a walk as his old hospital. Before, the nurse's station had been smack dab in the middle of a wing of thirteen curtains, with another thirteen on the other side. People were triaged in a small exam room, then they were given a bed until they were either admitted or discharged.

He'd been told there were twenty-five beds total in Hidden Creek Memorial, and that was split between urgent or acute care and patients who were recovering from the occasional procedure—a rarity in the hospital, and usually only occurring after an emergency.

Though most of the beds were for walk-ins, the layout wasn't especially efficient. There were only five curtains sectioning off little "rooms" for each patient, with another five down the hall, and more past that.

Curtain three was close to the nurse's station, though, and Kyle stopped outside the space, his blue sneakers—the one part of his wardrobe he got to choose as a nurse—peeked out under the curtain.

"Mind some company?" he asked, waiting for an answer before he drew back the curtain and stepped into the room.

He ignored the chart for a moment, focusing on the patient. She was in her late thirties, early forties if he had to guess, though the dark circles under her eyes and the deepened frown lines prob-ably made her look older than she was.

"I'm Kyle Harris, one of the on-duty nurses for today. I know you've probably talked to a bunch of people already, but I just wanted to touch base and find out what's going on. Maybe there's some way I can help?"

She squinted as she looked up at him, in obvious pain though she offered a friendly smile. "Brenda Carson," she said, introducing herself without the need for a chart. "You're right, I have talked to what seems like everybody in this damn hospital. Everybody but the one doctor who apparently works here. I know it's busy," her words dripped with sarcasm since both the beds beside hers were empty, "but I'd like to know what's causing these headaches sometime before Christmas."

Not a friendly smile, then. More of a "bless your heart" smile. But Kyle had long ago learned how to be patient and show compassion to people who were in pain or showing signs of distress.

"You know what, I will check on that for you. In the meantime, I'd like to ask a few questions, see for myself what's going on, if that's okay?"

With a heavy sigh, Brenda consented, and Kyle finally picked up her very much not digital chart. He'd brought a pen, thank God, because he didn't think the patient would've waited for him to rummage around for one.

As it was, he had a hard time getting answers out of her that weren't tinged with annoyance, but he was able to sift through the complaints to take down useful notes for the physician.

He'd guessed the migraines were keeping her up at night, and they were obviously making her more irritable. One of the other nurses had turned off the overhead light, but Kyle took the initiative to turn off the monitors and cover up every other light source, too.

"Any better?" he asked.

"Much," she said, bringing her hand down from her eyes. "Thank you. That beeping was going to drive me to drink."

"Afraid I'm all out of bourbon," Kyle said with a grin, "but I can fetch you a soda. The caffeine might help."

Maybe a cloth soaked in cool water, too. It wasn't as good as medication, but he wasn't authorized to write any prescriptions, only to dispense them. That was one of the reasons he'd decided to go back to school to become a physician's assistant. He hated feeling helpless when it came to patient care.

Brenda never had a chance to answer him, though, because the curtain was drawn back and a tall, well-built man entered. A tall, well-built man with a very familiar voice.

"Are you suggesting caffeine to my patient before she's had a workup done?"

Kyle stopped in his tracks, his eyes widening. It couldn't be. There was no fucking way. But the instant he turned around, he saw the man.

Wes was a doctor at Hidden Creek Memorial. Worse than that, Wes—the man who'd been kind and supportive when Kyle had blue-balled him last night—was the arrogant asshole all the other nurses warned him about.

6

WES

*O*f course Kyle was a nurse. The universe liked fucking with him too much for the man he'd taken home to be anything else.

Shame on him for never asking, he supposed, but he made it a rule never to talk about work when he was in the process of getting someone back to his bed. The people who found his medical degree a turn-on weren't people he wanted to fuck, and everybody else probably wouldn't care one way or the other. It wasn't like Wes was trying to impress anyone's parents. He'd gone all in for that once and never planned to do it again.

As far as Kyle was concerned, Wes had learned there was a new nurse when he checked in. Hidden Creek Memorial was a small hospital with an even smaller staff, and one of the nurses had retired almost a month ago, leaving a scheduling gap—and more importantly, a patient care gap—that needed to be filled. He'd barked to Sloane about it, and apparently the man finally found someone.

That someone just happened to be the sexy, heartbroken young newcomer he'd almost fucked the previous night.

Walking the halls, he'd heard Kyle's voice as he spoke to Ms. Carson. It stilled Wes in his tracks, but he recovered moments later. No one needed to see that he was affected by a member of staff. The people that worked at Hidden Creek were like vultures when it came to him, ready and willing to swoop down and pick apart what was left if he ever gave them the chance.

So he kept composed, and carefully avoided considering the travesty that was Kyle's ass covered in loose-fitting scrub pants.

"Afraid I'm all out of bourbon," the man said, grinning like a fool, "but I can fetch you a soda. The caffeine might help."

"Are you suggesting caffeine to my patient before she's had a workup done?"

Kyle turned immediately, his eyes widening slightly. He was obviously shocked, but that only seemed to last a moment before he shook himself out of it and returned his attention to his patient.

"I'm sorry for the wait, Ms. Carson." Wes' whole demeanor changed, the way it always did when he spoke to patients. No matter their condition, no matter how insignificant the case might seem to the staff, these people were terrified and looking for someone to make their case the most important thing on their docket. "I've told the nurses to page me if a consult is needed before morning rounds, but apparently they've had other priorities."

Brenda looked at the rows of empty beds on either side of her, her brow creasing in irritation. "Yeah, I can see that."

He felt Kyle staring at him, and knew it was with incredulity. But he ignored the man and moved beside his patient's bed. "You're here because of a persistent migraine, right? How long have you had it?"

He asked her a series of questions, not bothering to review the history Kyle or any of the other nurses had taken—if they'd taken one at all. There was an art to getting an accurate and helpful patient history, and Wes knew exactly the questions to ask to get the answers he needed. Questions about family history, the location of the migraines, her general pain level, auras and known triggers, if there was any nausea or other symptoms present, and more.

Kyle, however, didn't seem content with Wes' questioning. "How's your diet been lately?"

He shot the man a look, prepared to step in, but the patient was already answering.

"I don't know, the usual," Brenda said. "Are you going to harp on me for eating out, too?"

"No, he's not, because his idle curiosity has nothing to do with why you're suffering," Wes responded, preparing to move on.

"Diet actually plays a big part in our health, and certain foods might be a trigger for you. I'm not trying to put you on the spot, Ms. Carson, I just want to—"

"I'd like to get a CT scan," Wes cut in, "and some bloodwork done. We can treat your pain today, but I'd also like to find out what's causing these migraines and nip it in the bud."

Once Brenda consented he stepped outside, marking down the orders for the CT and the other tests he'd suggested. Kyle immediately followed him out, and when Wes looked over at him, the man's face was pinched in irritation. It made those soft lips of his stick out enticingly, but other than that, the expression did him a disservice.

"Can I speak with you? Doctor?" the last was said without the tone that usually accompanied the word, but there certainly wasn't any respect there.

"If you make it quick. I still have three follow-ups to do before I can actually start my day." Wes clicked his pen and slid it back into the pocket of his coat. So many doctors had stopped wearing them completely, opting for shirts and ties instead, but he wasn't interested in looking like he had a big meeting with the pharma reps to sit in on. He'd gone through hell to get that MD after his name and he was going to own it.

Kyle led him to one of the empty exam rooms, closing the door once Wes was inside. He arched a brow at the younger man, his thoughts running away with him despite the obvious conflict. For the most part, Wes kept his personal life separate from his professional life, but Kyle's pouty, self-righteous glare was doing strange things to him. His dick took notice of the privacy they were afforded here, despite the very thin walls, and he couldn't help but imagine how this might play out if Kyle had stayed just a bit longer last night.

They'd get into what was obviously about to be some heated disagreement. Tempers would flare, stoking a passion that was buried just below the surface. Too worked up to speak, Kyle would grip the hair at the nape of Wes' neck hard enough to sting, then he'd pull the man down for a hungry kiss. Cabinets would rattle as he pushed Kyle up against them, medical supplies clattering to the floor. His coat would be the first casualty. Then Kyle's scrub top...

"Was there a point to ordering so many unnecessary tests," Kyle began, very rudely pulling Wes out of his fantasy, "or are you just eager to bury her under a heap of medical bills her insurance won't pay?"

If the first statement hadn't sobered him, that certainly would have. Had a nurse ever talked to him like that before? Even when he was a wide-eyed medical student, he hadn't been taken to task in such a fashion. Kyle's attitude and insubordination were something that needed to be dealt with, but again all his horny mind could manage was the thought of taking the man over his knee and turning that tight, pert ass of his a lovely shade of red.

God, what was wrong with him? There was every chance Kyle had played him from the start. He probably knew exactly who Wes was, and he'd purposefully denied him last night. Now he was going all out to question Wes' judgment at every turn in hopes of humiliating him in front of the other nurses at some point. It seemed all too plausible, and Wes' temper flared.

"The point, Mr. Harris, is that Brenda Carson has a family history of cancer—"

"Which is why we should keep an eye on her, not saddle her with tests she doesn't need right now," Kyle interrupted.

"—And she was displaying other symptoms, some less subtle than others. The irritability, for one. Her balance was off, as well. You would've noticed, had you not been gaping at me."

"The irritability was because she had to wait so long while she was in pain, and the loss of balance could've been from a million other things," Kyle countered, not rising to the bait Wes had set out for him. "There's no reason to give her a full work-up until we see her lab results."

Well, Kyle certainly knew his diagnostics. It was a curious thing, and one that didn't help Wes' strange mix of suspicious and lustful feelings.

"She could die of an aneurysm before then," he fired back, "but it's good to know your priorities lay with efficiency rather than saving lives."

The look Kyle shot him could have frozen over hell itself, though it had the decidedly opposite effect of setting Wes' whole body afire. His coat suddenly felt stifling, and this room was far too small.

"I know what you're doing, and it's not going to work."

Some invisible force pulled him toward the indignant man, even as his conscious mind was aware it was a bad idea. Kyle held his gaze and Wes stopped mere inches away from him, looking down at his new co-worker. For the briefest second, Wes saw a furious heat light through Kyle's eyes that had nothing to do with his anger over Wes' patient care.

So he isn't completely unaffected. Maybe last night was just a fluke after all...

"What am I doing?" he murmured, his voice a low rumble. The slight, almost imperceptible shiver that raced through Kyle was far more gratifying than he'd expected.

"Trying to scare me; put me in my place on day one." Oh, Wes was eager to put Kyle in his place, but not in the way he meant. "It's not going to work. I'm not going to let you intimidate me just because you've had your hand on my cock."

"I'm just doing what's in the best interest of my patient, Mr. Harris. It really doesn't have anything to do with you, but I'm flattered you think that."

"Then why are you inches away from a sexual harassment claim?" Kyle hissed, demonstrating those inches very clearly, his mouth so close Wes could feel the heat of his breath.

But the man's words did wonders to snuff out the sudden, raging fire of want. Wes stepped back, smoothing down his white coat with one hand. He saw Kyle let out a held breath, and the tension in the room dissipated. The sexual tension, at least. The professional tension still remained, thick enough to slice through with a knife.

"If it concerns you, I can speak to the director," Wes said. "Tell him you and I had an… encounter, before you started working here, but that it's not going to be an issue. It's best to get ahead of these things before it's all over the hospital."

Kyle looked him over as though he were reconsidering, and that desire hummed to life again just beneath Wes' skin. What was it about this man in particular? He'd always maintained hard boundaries at work, and there was absolutely no universe in which he'd ever fuck someone in the hospital. But he wanted Kyle, and if the man had been willing to turn their disagreement into something more productive…

"Fine," Kyle said, then he belatedly added, "thanks. Thank you." He sighed, seeming to lose confidence with every breath. Long fingers swept through his sandy brown hair. "I'm sorry. I don't want to start this off with us arguing over what's best for a patient."

"It's good that you care," Wes admitted.

"Do you really think the other nurses don't?"

"Well, none of them saw fit to page me, thus making Ms. Carson spend hours of time in unnecessary pain. Sounds like they put their personal comfort above hers," he said with a pleasant smile that didn't match what he felt about the subject.

Kyle actually seemed to consider that, but Wes' patience for this whole situation was long gone, and he was a little afraid of what might happen if he stayed locked in a room with that man.

Reaching for the doorknob, he gave one last command, "Radiology takes their lunch early. Make sure you get that order in soon, or she'll be waiting even longer."

The look of annoyance Kyle shot him set the world on its axis again, and Wes slipped out to tend to his duties.

MORNING ROUNDS TOOK A BIT LONGER THAN HE'D EXPECTED, AND he didn't make it to Director Sloane's office until half past nine. Located on the third floor, in what hospital staff not-so-fondly referred to as Admin Alley, Sloane's office was the most excessive by far. The money used to put in a window that showed off a quaint view of the town could have been used to buy more supplies, and the cost of refurnishing the office last year could have easily supported the new computers everyone had been asking for since the dawn of time.

But Wes wasn't here to tell Sloane how he should run his hospital. The man was a private investor, and as such, he had final say. Considering Wes had been on thin ice for a few disagreements in the past, he wasn't inclined to start something he couldn't finish.

"Sir?" he knocked on the open door, just for the sake of decorum. Even though Sloane was sitting at his desk and obviously not in a meeting.

"Come on in, Monroe." That old Texan accent blended his words together in a way Wes simultaneously admired for its uniqueness and also found a little difficult to understand—though he'd never admit it. "What can I do ya? You get the nurses' feathers all ruffled again?"

The casual misogyny was a lot less endearing. Especially when it wasn't overt enough that Wes could call him out on it. It was subtle, and it got under his skin. So much so that he had to wonder if people saw him the same way.

"Yes and no," he admitted, taking a seat unprompted. "I have to clear the air a bit. The newest hire, Kyle Harris. I met him at the bar last night, before I knew he'd be working here."

"So you fucked one of the nurses? That what you're telling me, son?"

No, there definitely wasn't anything endearing about the man's attitude. "I'm letting you know we had a personal relationship—however brief—before he started here. People talk in this town, and I'm sure someone saw me with him. I just wanted to get it out in the open before it became a bigger deal than it actually is."

"Look, as long as you aren't knocking boots in the middle of your shift, I don't care what you do or who you do it with." He sounded mildly annoyed, and added, "but I appreciate you lettin' me know."

Tom Sloane had never been the most progressive man on the planet. He just tolerated most people and said whatever he felt like saying at the time. But he didn't usually have this short of a fuse, and Wes took a moment to get a better look at the man. This close, he could see there were bags under Sloane's eyes and lines etched into his face that hadn't been there yesterday. Papers were strewn about his desk, along with two coffee cups and an empty can of Red Bull.

"You doing okay, Tom?" Wes asked tentatively.

"Well since you're asking, no, I'm sure as hell not. Look at all this shit." He gestured to the papers on his desk. "All this god damn paperwork over a simple deal. Used to be, if you wanted to do business with a man you just look him in the eye, shake his hand, and that'd be the end of it."

Wes wasn't sure it had ever been like that, with the exception of a few weekday syndicated shows that aired in the early sixties. Shows Tom wasn't old enough to have watched outside of reruns. But it was obvious the man had entered the realm of hyperbole. The more he swore, the deeper he went down the rabbit hole.

"What deal? You and June finally find somebody to buy the house?"

Tom barked a dry laugh. "I wish. Least that'd be over and done with once all this shit was signed." He sighed, scratching his fingers through his graying beard. "No, this is... Ah, hell." He looked up at Wes, an oddly guilty expression tucked within his brown eyes. "Look: The county's offered to buy the hospital's assets. You know, equipment and whatnot."

For a second, Wes felt like the man was just messing with him. A cruel joke in poor taste, but a joke nonetheless. Sloane didn't look amused in the slightest, though. He still looked guilty, and he couldn't quite meet Wes' gaze.

"What exactly does that mean?" Wes asked, hoping he was just overreacting.

Maybe Tom needed to cut back on non-essentials, though he couldn't think what that would possibly be. There were already lines for most of the testing equipment and a huge backup in the labs.

"It means I have to close down the hospital." A cold, clammy feeling washed over Wes. "Now don't look at me like that. I've been limping along for years. Decades. You know that. I'm out of options here, Wes. Either I sell what I can, or June and I lose everything." The older man looked around his desk as if trying to pinpoint a hidden bottle of bourbon. All he found was a water bottle. "I'm not just thinking of myself, here. I've put in a good word with the county hospitals. I'm working on finding places for everybody."

"I don't understand. What about the fundraisers a few years back? The re-financing? The money supposedly coming in from the bank?" he asked, his agitation growing.

"Do you know how much it costs to keep this place operational, Wes? I'm tapped out. Have been for a while. I just… didn't want to see it."

"You just hired a new nurse!" he shot back.

"That was before I had a nice, long sit-down with my accountant. Back when I still thought I could hire a couple more people, fix the efficiency problems, and the rest would sort itself out."

Wes' lips pressed into a thin line, his jaw clenching. Even if that was the truth, it wasn't justification to pull the rug out from under everyone. There was far more at stake than Sloane's finances.

"What about our patients? Where are they supposed to go?"

"The county hospital's more than equipped—" Sloane began.

"The county hospital's run like a fucking assembly line. They just shove patients through the motions and discharge them as quickly as they can. You can't do this to them, Tom. You can't do this to Hidden Creek."

There was a reason he'd come back to Hidden Creek after his residency was over. City hospitals were never at a loss for staff and they never would be. But rural hospitals got the short end of the stick in so many ways, and Wes at least wanted to make sure the people of his hometown received adequate care. Now he wouldn't even be able to do that anymore.

"Here's the long and short of it," Sloane said, leaning his elbows on his desk. "Hidden Creek Memorial's dug itself too big of a hole. I can't sustain this place, and I'm out of chances with all my lenders.

I have to close, Wes. I need a fighting chance at getting my head above water, here."

"And the people who come through these doors want a fighting chance at life, not a thirty to forty-minute ambulance ride just to be seen," he grated out.

Sloane's face turned hard, his brown eyes looking a lot less friendly than they normally did. Drawing his elbows off of the table, he organized the chaotic mess of papers into a stack, barely looking at Wes as he said, "It's out of your hands, Dr. Monroe. It's about time you learned there's some things you can't control, no matter how much you want to."

7

WES

*W*es kept himself up most of the night spinning scenarios through his head. Scenarios in which he could somehow stop Tom from closing the hospital.

Were he living in an ideal world, he would have rallied the staff and relied on several perspectives, not just his own. But the rest of the staff barely communicated with him regarding matters of life and death. They weren't going to cooperate on this. Most likely they'd panic and devote all of their time to looking for new jobs, leaving Hidden Creek completely in the lurch.

Until Tom decided to announce it—which probably wouldn't be until everything was official, considering how Wes had reacted—he'd just keep all this to himself. He could split his time between working his normal shifts and figuring out how to turn this around. It would require a lot less sleep, but he'd worked on fewer hours during his first year of residency. Getting three consecutive hours a night was a luxury back then. He just needed to readjust. And invest in a coffee press.

So far, though—without the coffee press or time to readjust his sleep cycles—Wes hadn't come up with anything useful. He'd written down "find and marry a rich lesbian heiress," but that had mostly been for his own amusement, and part of a longstanding joke he shared with Doris, the woman who'd essentially been like a mother to him after his own passed. While it cheered him up to think of her, it'd been almost four in the morning when he'd written down that particular solution, and he hadn't thought she'd appreciate the text to let her know he was finally going to take her advice.

The next three hours had only soured his mood, and when he walked into Hidden Creek Memorial at seven, he wasn't inclined to play the office politics game. He ignored the frantic whispering that stopped the moment he walked by and dropped off his things in his locker. The doctor who'd been on duty overnight—Sharon Silverman—briefed him on the patients that were waiting for morning rounds.

None of those patients included Brenda Carson, which was both a blessing and a curse. After several rounds of inconclusive testing, he'd been forced to discharge her with a prescription and a suggestion to follow up with her primary care doctor for long term care. He'd felt like it wasn't enough, but there'd been no way to prove there was anything wrong with the woman beyond what just seemed to be a textbook case of rebound headaches. Kyle had digested that news with all the smugness Wes expected. Not outwardly so. He was polite, and he put Ms. Carson's needs first. But there'd been a moment when Wes was signing the discharge papers that he swore he saw the man give a very obvious "I told you so" look.

That was yesterday, though, and today he had bigger things to worry about than some squabble with a man he'd almost fucked. He'd let Kyle know the director had been notified of their previous relationship, and that was all they needed to talk about on a personal level. Everything else needed to remain firmly grounded in their work, because Wes really didn't need to devote the extra brainpower to these ridiculous fantasies he had whenever Kyle was near.

Fantasies that didn't stop just because they were inconvenient. His very first follow-up was also a patient Harris happened to be taking vitals for. Just seeing him—the way his whole demeanor softened as he spoke to the older woman, and conversely how every muscle in his body seemed to tense when he noticed Wes' presence—made him fixate on things he shouldn't.

Wes would never claim to have a type, but his last relationship had been with the most stubborn man he'd ever met, and his moms loved to tease him to the point of discomfort about the virtues of a testy partner.

"Good morning, Mrs. Hartford," he said, reaching for the woman's chart. "Dr. Silverman said you're still having some trouble breathing?"

"It's not so bad," she lied, in direct defiance of what Silverman's observations said. "I've spent a lot more time breathing than doing anything else. I figure my lungs just need a little break."

Kyle laughed softly at that as he maneuvered the head of a stethoscope under a blood pressure cuff. "You should look into becoming the next Bionic Woman. You could get everything regulated that way."

"Wouldn't have to worry about pesky little things like breathing, then!" she said with a toothy grin, gesticulating as she did so. Kyle had the patience not to tell her to keep her arm still while he was trying to get a pressure read. "Plus I'd get to have a torrid affair with Richard Anderson..."

"That sounds even better than cybernetic modification," Wes

admitted, glancing at Kyle over the woman's chart. The hint of a smile made him feel ridiculously victorious.

"Don't I know it," Mrs. Hartford said with a wistful sigh.

"In the meantime, while we wait for science to catch up, I'd like to take a listen to your lungs," he said, getting out his own stethoscope.

"Let me know if they say anything too crass. Ornery little fuckers."

Wes bit down on his lip, willing himself not to laugh. It took even more of an effort when he could see Kyle doing the exact same thing. They moved around one another fluidly, without Wes having to say anything. He just waited for Kyle to finish taking the BP, then they traded places seamlessly. Rubbing the metal end of the stethoscope against his hand to warm it up, Wes placed it on the woman's back.

"Deep breath for me." When she did as he instructed, he followed it up with, "And let it out."

This was repeated two more times, as Kyle took a pulse ox. There was clear wheezing present, and Mrs. Hartford's breathing was more shallow than it should be. Dr. Silverman's diagnosis of COPD definitely seemed correct. She'd explained they'd kept the woman for observation overnight to see if she continued to have issues after being given a dose of steroids.

Well that was… surprisingly pleasant. Wes left with a smile on his face and a lightness in his step that he couldn't completely contribute to Mrs. Hartford's sense of humor—though that certainly helped. It was rare that he'd ever found himself in sync with another medical professional. Even the doctors he'd worked alongside had their own style that tended to throw him off his game. It was a large part of why he'd decided against becoming a surgeon.

But something seemed to click in that room. Kyle understood the patient's needs as well as Wes did, if not better. Rather miraculous, considering they'd both just started their shifts. He had a knack for reading people, and his desire to make his patients comfortable was evident in everything he did. It made Wes feel like he could leave that room and only come back when it was absolutely necessary, content in the knowledge that someone else would actually handle it properly.

And that was insane to him, honestly. He'd always checked in on his patients as often as he could. He knew firsthand what could happen if someone wasn't doing their job; if a patient needed something but was unable to ask for it. But Mrs. Hartford was in good hands, and he moved on to the next case with a clear conscience.

Or he would have, if he hadn't caught the latest gossip coming from the nurses' station.

"I'm telling you, Monroe didn't snap at him once. They spent the whole time laughing and carrying on with the patient," Vivian said. "Whole thing was surreal."

"So what, is this some sort of male bonding thing? He and the new guy are laughing it up while he treats the women like we're toddlers?"

Wes drew in a breath through his nose, so tempted to correct them immediately. They must have known he could hear. It wasn't like he was skulking about. He'd walked right past the station and had just turned the corner when they started going off.

"I think it's more than that. I don't know for sure, but I've seen the way Kyle looks at him..."

That put things into sharp perspective. This was just hospital gossip and backwoods politics—two things he didn't have time for today. The crushing weight of Sloane's decision came back with a vengeance, and it took a Herculean effort to shake off the mood he found himself in before he drew back the curtain for bed eight. Speaking to that patient and the next helped ground him. But before he could even greet his fourth of the day—a young boy who'd come down with some kind of stomach bug and was severely dehydrated—Wes' pager went off.

One glance at the code was enough to send him running out of the room, a hasty apology on his lips as he raced toward seven— Mrs. Hartford's room.

There were some doctors who thrived under this kind of pressure, but Wes had never been one of them. A code was a failure, especially when it happened while he was tending to someone else. A code on an otherwise stable patient usually meant someone had fucked up along the way and something had gone terribly wrong—to the point where it might cost a patient their life.

When he turned the corner, he saw it was curtain seven everyone was flocking to, and that made the feelings charging through him even worse. Mrs. Hartford had a simple, treatable problem. She shouldn't be in this situation, period.

"What happened?" he barked, throwing back the curtain.

"She was looking pale and listless, so I tried to engage her in conversation and she just started convulsing."

There was no panic in the Kyle's voice as he said it, and Wes was grateful for small miracles. A panicked nurse wasn't going to help anyone right now, least of all Mrs. Hartford.

"BP's dropping," Gina, one of the other nurses said. "She's going into asystole."

Everything was happening so fast, and Wes had to retreat inside himself to do what was necessary to save this woman's life. He refused to lose a patient today. He wasn't going to do it, streak be damned. This was about the value of life, and Wes refused to let it slip through his fingers.

"Starting compressions," he yelled, and the rest of the staff cleared to the side of the bed for him. "Push 1mg epi, now."

Hands positioned, stance perfectly straight, Wes began CPR, pumping the woman's chest, checking for signs of a pulse, and then restarting.

As a kid, he'd always thought defibrillators were the first and last line of defense in saving people from death, but the reality was a lot more nuanced. There were some people who couldn't take the shock, and some who wouldn't be affected by it in the slightest. In general, with patients who'd had heart complications in the past, Wes preferred to treat with compressions and IV meds to kick the patient's heart back into an acceptable rhythm.

It was damage control—a Band-Aid until he could find out what had actually gone wrong and what kind of havoc it was currently wreaking on her body.

But it was a gambit that worked. Between the meds and the compressions, Mrs. Hartford's pulse registered again. The flurry of chaos didn't stop then, though. They needed to make sure she was stable, and Wes needed to figure out what suddenly made his stable patient go into full-on cardiac arrest.

"What the hell happened?" he asked, his fury directed right at Kyle.

He was the one in charge of the patient's care. He had to know.

"Everything you ordered happened," Kyle shot back. "I gave her pseudoephedrine 30mg—"

"You gave her *what*?" he roared. "You gave pseudoephedrine to a woman who's already suffering from heart disease?!"

Kyle blanched, finally stepping away from the gurney as the others worked. "You wrote it down. You wrote down pseudoephedrine. And her chart never said anything about—"

"Get the labetalol," he barked at another nurse. "We need to get her BP down."

"What can I do?" Kyle asked, looking pale and frantic.

"Go literally anywhere else," Wes growled, "and try not to cause another fucking code."

THE PROCESS OF SAVING MRS. HARTFORD WAS DRAWN OUT MORE than Wes would have liked, but in the end, they managed to stabilize her. She'd even regained consciousness in the last hour and seemed to have full use of her faculties, which was always a concern after someone was down for any length of time.

It should have felt like a relief, but all Wes could think was that they'd failed the patient. That he'd failed the patient, because apparently he should have been babysitting Kyle to make sure he administered the right prescriptions.

Wes was still seething by the time he sought out the man. He knew he should've taken some time to cool off, maybe had a little jog around town to clear his head, but this couldn't be left to fester. Kyle needed to know that these kinds of mistakes were unacceptable.

He found the man at the nurses' station, staring at the ancient computer with a look of distinct frustration pinching his face. Was he having a hard day? Because Wes was about to make it a hundred times harder.

"I need to go over the Hartford case with you," he said as evenly as he could manage.

Even if his anger threatened to boil over, he wasn't going to dress someone down in public. Once they were behind closed doors, though...

"That's what I'm looking at now," Kyle said, not even turning his attention to Wes. "Nowhere in her file does it say she has heart disease."

A cold feeling washed over Wes, and he bent down to look at the eyesore of a monitor. "Show me."

Kyle scrolled through Mrs. Hartford's file, pointing out the place where the procedure should have been listed. Various procedures were listed, but the diagnosis of heart disease wasn't anywhere to be found.

"I took her history myself," he said, taken aback. "I would've put it in the system."

"Then there's a problem with the electronic filing system," Kyle said, pushing his chair back.

Wes just stared at him incredulously. "That's it? 'There's a problem with the electronic filing system?' That 'problem' almost cost a woman her life."

"I know that, Dr. Monroe," Kyle said through gritted teeth. "That's why I was going to speak to the director about getting it looked at by IT."

Considering Sloane currently had the same interest in this hospital as a rat did in a sinking ship, he knew nothing would be done about it. And that fact made him all the angrier.

"A faulty system doesn't explain how you misinterpreted my med order. I never told you to give Mrs. Hartford pseudoephedrine."

"Yes, you did," Kyle shot back, grabbing the physical chart from the desk and pointing to the order.

Wes looked down at the chart, dread gripping him. Had he really made this big of a mistake? Was he the only one responsible for almost killing Mrs. Hartford?

He knew he'd been tired, that last night had taken its toll, but this...

When he scanned the chart, though, all he saw was the order for prednisone.

"You mean here where I wrote down prednisone?" he asked, drawing in a steadying breath through his nose.

"This?" That one word was steeped in so much disbelief that Wes' confidence faltered. "This doesn't say prednisone. I can barely read the fucking thing," he hissed, his words low enough so only Wes could hear him, "but that's not what it says. The closest thing I got from it was pseudoephedrine, which I assumed was safe for her to take."

"You assumed?" Wes just stared at the man, at those mossy green eyes that had held such a captivating mystery before. Now they were filled with a stubborn self-righteousness mixed with a healthy dose of guilt. "So when Mrs. Hartford asks why she almost died in our hospital, I'm supposed to just tell her you assumed I wrote something and didn't bother to ask me?"

"As long as you don't leave out the part where you told me not to bother you unless it was urgent," Kyle shot back. "I made the wrong call. I own that. But this chicken scratch you call a med order is illegible, *doctor*."

"I guess we'll see how Sloane feels about it when the hospital's facing down a lawsuit for gross incompetence."

The chart hit the table with a heavy slap, and Wes removed himself from the nurses' station in three long strides, getting as far away from Kyle as he could manage.

It wasn't just that the man fought him on this, stirring his temper the way none of the other nurses dared to do.

It was the fact that he was right.

Even Wes wasn't positive what that drug order said, only what he'd intended. There was every chance in the world that fatigue and a hasty prescription had been at the heart of this whole situation, and that was on him. Not on Kyle. Not on an ancient computer system.

Him.

Ignoring everything and everyone around him, Wes stormed into the on-call room, locked the door behind him… and finally gave into the tears of stress and frustration and anger that had been threatening to strangle him since yesterday.

8

KYLE

_K_yle stood under the lukewarm shower, feeling bruised, battered, and absolutely defeated.

The bruising was to his pride, and the battering was more blistering than anything else. After Mrs. Hartford's code, he'd done everything in double time, and his new shoes had rubbed the back of his heels raw.

But the feeling of being completely defeated was a pervasive, all-over thing. It ran through his blood, soaked over him in every droplet of water, and wormed its way into his mind with the hiss of steam and the memory of Wes' words to him.

It would've been one thing if the man was just an arrogant asshole who liked blaming everything on nurses, but Kyle had made a mistake. He'd let Wes intimidate him, even when he said he wouldn't, and he'd let what could have been a two second annoyance become a life-threatening situation.

Yes, Dr. Monroe had the handwriting of a five-year-old, but that was no excuse. He knew better than to act off of assumption. Had he really let Wes get into his head that much?

Considering he was still thinking about all of this a good hour after leaving the hospital, the answer was apparently yes.

He'd told Brandon he'd meet him and Katie at Rocket for a late meal around eight thirty, but that had given Kyle almost a full hour to sit and feel sorry for himself before he bothered getting into the shower.

Even now, he was wasting time. It'd be a wonder if he made it to Rocket by eight thirty. But he just couldn't help replaying everything in his mind, like he was watching some sadistic highlight reel comprised of his biggest fuckups—and these were just the ones from the last few days.

He'd come to Hidden Creek for a change, but this feeling of being off-kilter and severely under-guarded around Wesley Monroe was not what he needed. And he definitely didn't need to start making dumb mistakes that would compromise patient care all because he couldn't talk to one man.

Dragging himself out of the shower, Kyle goes dressed and made his way out to the car before he could fill his mind with any other negative thoughts. He set the GPS for Rocket, made the surprisingly short drive, and locked up out of habit before heading inside.

While the massive pizza they'd had delivered just days before had come in a standard take-out pizza box, the diner itself was anything but ordinary. The whole thing was a throwback to the fifties with checkered tile floor, bright red leather upholstered booths and chairs, and lots of tacky sci-fi decorations that really hammered in the theme.

It was charming in a way Kyle hadn't expected, and it helped to at least divert his attention for a few moments. Seeing Katie waving to him from a booth in the back also helped, and he made his way over there.

"Hey, sorry I'm late," he said with an apologetic smile.

"Nah, you're not," Brandon assured him. "We're early. Katie's been pulling my arm to play the claw machine, but I told her not until after she'd eaten dinner."

Across from him, Katie gave her father one of the best puppy dog faces Kyle had ever seen. Apparently Brandon had some kind of innate resistance, because he just shook his head.

"Food first. You know the rule."

She sighed and settled into the booth, finally acting like what Kyle had expected a ten-year-old to act like.

Now, though, was the time small talk usually happened. Rather than talk about work, Kyle pulled up the menu, putting it squarely in front of his face. Even the menus followed the vintage sci-fi motif, and again he had to smile at the owner's dedication.

A teenaged waitress came by and Kyle went all out, ordering a patty melt and a root beer float. If he was going to sit down and eat at an old timey diner after a bad day, he was determined to stuff his face full of whatever comfort foods he wanted.

Brandon and Katie followed suit, and soon the menus were taken and there was nothing left but the obvious question. He could see it in Brandon's eyes as his brother looked at him.

"You look like hell, Ky. Long day?"

"Yeah," he said with a dry laugh, glancing at Katie. "Just busy. We had a John Doe come in from a car accident today. Tomorrow will be better."

It wasn't a lie, though it wasn't the full truth. Tomorrow had to be better because today was the bottom of the fucking barrel.

Brandon looked skeptical, considering Kyle for a long moment.

When it seemed his brother was on the verge of asking a follow-up question, Kyle took charge.

"You're home for the summer now, right?" he asked Katie. "Any big plans?"

Katie just shrugged a little, looking across the table at him with a shy smile. "Not really. I got my reading list for fourth grade. And Dad said we could start a garden this summer. We're going to go get the stuff for it from the Farmer's Market this weekend."

"Oh yeah? What are you going to grow?"

Katie rattled off a long list of flowers, fruits, vegetables, and herbs, some of which had Kyle realizing he was way hungrier than he realized. Had he eaten anything today? There'd been that granola bar he'd wolfed down in the middle of the day, but other than that…

"We're actually going to build a shed at some point to house all the tools, and as a place to put the starters if I can get a big enough window in there that faces the sun. Either that or some heat lamps."

His niece nodded enthusiastically, more excited about growing things than he'd been about anything else he'd ever done during summer vacation. Playing video games? Riding his bike up and down the road? Maybe the summer he'd finally gotten his learner's permit, but even that seemed like a stretch for how bouncy Katie was.

"Maybe you can come over and help us sometime?" she asked, turning the puppy dog eyes on him.

"Kyle works long hours, sweetie, and I'm sure he'll want to spend his days off relaxing."

Kyle wasn't sure what was worse: His brother's assumption or

Katie's immediate, crestfallen expression. But this was the precedent he'd set, wasn't it? And aside from forgetting about Rebecca and Mike, this was what he'd come to Hidden Creek to fix.

"I'll set some time aside for it. Just give me a week's notice, okay? So I can clear it with my boss."

Plans were made, and Katie was over the moon, practically vibrating out of her seat with excitement. Or maybe that was the soda. Their food came not too long after, and the three of them ate with limited chatter. Perfectly fine by Kyle, since he was afraid of what he'd say if given free rein. And the patty melt he'd bought was really, really good. The beef was fresh, the cheese was tangy and melty, and the bread was toasted just the way he liked it. The whole meal—onion rings and root beer float included—was probably a million calories, but he'd had a shit day, and if he couldn't spoil himself at a themed diner, where could he spoil himself?

Once Katie had finished her chicken fingers and french fries, most of her attention returned to the claw machine. Kyle swung a glance over his shoulder to get a look at this apparently prized piece of arcade nostalgia and found his eyes widening. Instead of the plastic and Plexiglas setups he was used to, this one seemed to be made of brass and actual, breakable glass. There was a bright patina on it, and he honestly wasn't sure if it was from age or if the owner of the diner had distressed it by hand.

The thing was impressive, either way, and he was tempted to join his niece once she got a handful of quarters out of her dad. He didn't have much interest in the stuffed animals—except for what looked like a rainbow-colored llama wedged in the corner—but he was itching to know how the thing worked. It looked like something from the Midway.

But as soon as Katie was off, Brandon took the opportunity to corner him. "So what's really going on? You look like you haven't slept in a week, Kyle."

A sarcastic remark rose to the tip of his tongue, but he didn't think pointing out the fact that Brandon probably didn't know him well enough to know when he looked tired seemed like really bad form, considering he'd been the one to leave. Letting out a heavy sigh, Kyle just decided to go with the truth. What was the worst that could happen?

"Work's been a bitch," he said, scrubbing a hand over his face. "We had a woman today, very sweet, very funny. She was being treated for COPD, which should've just been an in and out thing. A little monitoring just to be safe, but there was no reason she shouldn't have gone home before noon."

"What happened?" Brandon asked, his attention drifting briefly to Katie before he returned to Kyle.

"She ended up coding."

"Fuck." The horrified expression on Brandon's face told him just how often that happened at a small-town hospital. Great. This situation just kept getting better and better. "Is she...?"

"We saved her," Kyle said, his expression tight. "And when I left she was back to her old self. Cracking jokes, flirting with everyone on staff, the usual."

A fond smile touched his lips at that. He'd done his best to stay out of the way. It was obvious Wes didn't want him interfering, and honestly, Kyle didn't trust himself not to fuck something up. Nothing had ever rattled his confidence so bad. But he'd heard her talking when he passed by, and gossip about just who she'd hit on—and what she said to them—spread through the small hospital quickly, so he'd at least had that to hold on to.

"Jesus. You could've led with that. Who was it? Wait, no. Don't tell me. It has to be Mrs. Hartford." Brandon laughed. "Nobody else would try to pick up a date after almost dying."

"You know I can't tell you that," he said with a smile. "And sorry. It just... it never should've happened, is what I'm getting at. But wires got crossed and now we're at each other's throats and—"

"We?" Brandon's brows lifted.

"This doctor. Wes Monroe."

Even saying the man's name filled him with a host of mixed feelings, not all of them bad. But they were definitely all... intense.

"Ah, yeah. That'll do it. I should've warned you about him. Apparently none of the nurses can stand him." His brother shrugged and picked up his iced tea, gnawing lightly on the straw with the corner of his mouth. "He was good with Katie when I brought her in for vaccines."

"His bedside manner is something that should be studied by medical schools around the country," Kyle admitted, "but he's just a dick to everyone else. But... it wasn't just him being an arrogant ass this time, Bran. I really fucked up."

Brandon stopped torturing the poor straw, one dark brow arching as he waited for Kyle to explain. Letting out a heavy breath—and shooting a wistful glance to what remained of his root beer float—Kyle started from the beginning.

"You remember the night we were at Bottom's Up, how there was a gap of time between you going home to check on Katie and you coming to pick me up?" Brandon just nodded. "A guy came over to me right after you left. He started flirting with me, talking really suggestively, and change sounded good at the time, so... I went home with him."

Kyle's brother leaned back against the booth's bench like he'd been knocked back by a gust of air. "Wait. You went home with a guy?"

"Yeah, I know. Hooking up with strangers isn't usually my thing, but again. Changes. Plus... I don't know. There was something about him that just drew me in, and..." Kyle took in his brother's still-present look of surprise and realized why this seemed like such a big deal. "And that's not the surprising part of this story."

"Don't get me wrong," Brandon said hurriedly, putting his hands up in defense. "I think it's great. I had no idea you were bi, that's all."

"Neither did I. And I mean, I'm not sure if I am or not," he admitted. "I just... know I was attracted to him."

It wasn't like being attracted to men was something he'd absolutely run from, he'd just never really felt it before. Something about Wes hit him hard, and he'd found himself infatuated like a hormone-riddled teenager within minutes of meeting the man. Maybe he should have analyzed it; agonized over the newfound aspect of his sexuality that he hadn't become acquainted with until he was nearing thirty. But... why?

He was attracted to men. So what? As far as Kyle was concerned, the only thing that changed was his options for a partner, either casually or as something long-term. He was still the same person. He still wanted the same things out of his life and relationships. And if anyone decided to treat him differently because he'd suddenly realized he was bi... well, that was their problem, not Kyle's.

Right now, the identity of the man he'd gone home with was a much more pressing matter. He'd gotten sidetracked, and he quickly tried to tie in this whole story. "It was Wes. The man I went home with was Dr. Monroe."

Brandon let out a low whistle, his brows lifting as though he were impressed by the extraordinary feat of bad luck. "That's some *General Hospital* level scandal right there. So you banged the doctor you're working with, and now things are weird?"

"What?" Kyle asked, heat rising in his cheeks. "I didn't... we didn't..." He rolled his eyes at himself. He was a grown ass man. No reason to tiptoe around it. "I wasn't ready to take that step, so we didn't. Wes was kind and considerate and just a completely different person from who he turned out to be at work. So now there's that weirdness between us and I'm just not sure how to approach him, Bran."

He wasn't going to tell his brother that it was hard to have work conversations with a man who'd had his hand on Kyle's dick. That seemed a bit too much sharing for their current sibling bond. It wasn't even the crux of the issue, either.

"It's like he's two completely different people. The guy I met—the guy who takes such good care of his patients—and this asshole who wouldn't know humility if it hit him in the face."

Brandon snorted, though his expression was guarded, even wary, as he looked at Kyle. "You're not going to like my advice."

"At this point, I'll take anything. Even if you're going to tell me to just go home with him again and get it out of my system." Whoa. Where had that come from? More importantly, had Brandon noticed?

The look he got from across the table—the slight twitch of his brother's lips—definitely confirmed that he had, even before he said the words. "Is that on the table?"

"Pff. No," Kyle sputtered, lacing his fingers through his messy hair. "Shut up. What was your idea?"

Brandon laughed, a sound that helped ease Kyle's sudden bout of nerves. This was nice. This was exactly what he'd come to Hidden Creek to get back—his relationship with his brother. And if they had to bond over Kyle's blunders, then that was one he was willing to take for the team.

"I think you need to take the high road here. You both made mistakes, but I'm not sure having some kind of a stand-off over who was more wrong is going to help anything," Brandon said.

Kyle's eyes fell closed, a sigh slipping past his lips. When he opened his eyes again, his attention fell on Katie. She'd just sunk another quarter into the machine and was trying to line up the drop.

"So you think I should apologize," he said softly. "Try to be the bigger man."

"If he were anyone else, wouldn't you do the same thing?" Brandon had a point there. He'd let his ideas about who Wes was —both what he'd seen the night before he started working at the hospital, and what he'd learned from the other nurses—color his perception of the man.

Yes, he was an ass. But he was also the hospital's biggest advocate for patient care. That much was obvious to Kyle from day one, and in that goal, the two of them were aligned. The apology and the reasoning behind it practically wrote itself.

"Yeah. You're right," Kyle said, though not as grudgingly as he'd expected. "We need a clean slate."

If Wes insisted on putting him down—or pinning him with those intense stares—afterward, then at least he could say he'd tried. But for now Kyle was going to do his job, put his patients first, and try not to think about Dr. Wesley Monroe more than was absolutely necessary.

9

KYLE

*ew day. New attitude. New set of circumstances to be anxious about.

After his conversation with Brandon, Kyle had resolved to take the high road and apologize for his part in what happened to Mrs. Hartford. Whether Wes accepted the apology or changed his behavior didn't matter—at least, that was what he tried to convince himself. What mattered was that he didn't want to give Wes, or anyone else, the very wrong idea that he was just as arrogant and unable to put the patient's needs before his own.

As he walked into the hospital a good half hour before his shift, though, he couldn't help thinking it would all be for nothing. The tense work environment that had been present from day one would still be there. Wes would still see him as a liability. Someone he had to tolerate, but who wasn't an actual asset to patient care.

Why do you care what he thinks?

In the grand scheme of things, he didn't. If Wes wanted to believe all nurses were second-rate medical professionals, fine. There were plenty of doctors who shared that opinion. What bothered Kyle was the worry that he, specifically, wasn't making enough of an impact to be seen. Not by Wes, necessarily, but by anyone. His colleagues, his boss, the patients.

It was a fear that had manifested back in nursing school, when he'd jumped on every lab and internship opportunity he could get just to prove some theoretical "them" wrong.

No. It wasn't just nursing school. It started well before that, when his mom told him—after downing a fifth of vodka—that he wasn't going to amount to anything. He was too soft. Too sensitive. He let people walk all over him, and he was going to spend his life as the eager to please 'yes man' nobody ever remembered.

Kyle stopped just past the automated doors, that memory catching him off guard. He hadn't thought about his mom in years. Not consciously, anyway. Not since his father's funeral, when he'd seen the pictures of her that showed the bright, vivacious woman she was—when she wasn't drinking.

He drew in a breath through his nose and soldiered on. That was something to untangle some other day, when he had the mental fortitude to deal with it. For now, he needed to psych himself up. Wes would be in soon, and Kyle needed to sort out exactly what he'd say to the man.

Greeting the nurses who were finishing up their shifts from the night before, he made his way to the break room and popped open his locker. No sooner had he stashed his valuables and grabbed his kit than the door swung open, a wide stride eating up the tile floor behind him.

Somehow, Kyle instinctively knew it was Wes. It was that hair-raising feeling he'd always felt right before a Texas thunderstorm.

He turned to see Wes popping open the back off the coffee maker. The man made a face at the very dirty filter, but tossed it without comment. Considering he hadn't gone on some immediate tirade about how the night shift nurses never remembered to make a fresh pot for the day crew—something he'd admittedly heard his colleagues bitch about—Kyle decided this was the best mood he was going to find Wes in, and went for it.

"Hey." Solid start. Especially when the doctor didn't acknowledge him beyond a clipped glance. "I wanted to talk to you for a minute. About Mrs. Hartford's case."

"She was discharged last night," Wes said. "She'll be following up with her PCP next week, and her son is going to come stay with her for a few days until she feels better."

He still didn't look at Kyle. He just washed out the coffee maker and the carafe, pulled down some paper towels to dry everything, then seated a new filter inside.

Meanwhile, Kyle was left wondering how he'd found that out when he just got in. But that wasn't the point of this conversation. He already knew Wes was intensely focused on patient care. Now he needed to prove that he was, too. At least enough to put this whole thing behind them.

"That's great to hear," he said, somewhat awkwardly. The whole thing was made even more awkward by the fact that his badge got caught in his locker and he had to yank it out.

Wes, of course, hadn't noticed.

Kyle felt his temper rising. It was impossible not to think this was some kind of power play on the man's part. But he was reminded of his brother's words, and he finally came out with it.

"I messed up," he began, letting out a breath. "I should have asked for clarification on the med order before I administered anything. I was so worked up over the shitty way you were suddenly treating me that I did exactly what I told you I wouldn't. I let you intimidate me, and the patient suffered because of it."

It didn't feel as good to get that off his chest as he'd hoped. Probably because, as he'd said, someone paid for his inability to separate his job from his bruised ego. Of course, it didn't help that Wes all but whirled on him, a savage look in his eyes that Kyle just knew was going to lead to a knock-down, drag-out argument in the middle of the break room.

But something changed. Wes' expression settled, the anger lines easing, the fury dying down. Steel grey eyes searched his, and the doctor's expression eased even further at what they found there. After several moments of silence, he just looked... indescribably tired.

Honestly, Wes looked like he hadn't slept in a week. Even the slight nod he gave spoke of a bone-deep fatigue, and Kyle had to stop himself from asking questions.

"Thankfully the consequences weren't as dire as they could have been," Wes said, flipping the switch on the coffee maker. "Just don't let it happen again."

Kyle bit back his most immediate response. Wes wasn't his boss, and he definitely didn't have the authority to treat him like an underling. But what would arguing that point accomplish? Wes wasn't saying anything he didn't already know.

Still, after much deliberation, Kyle decided to be just a little bit petty. "Right. Good talk."

Part of him expected Wes to rise to the bait, but there was nothing. The doctor just waited for the slow-drip coffee maker without saying a word or otherwise acknowledging Kyle's presence.

Well. That was a waste of everyone's time, he thought. Wes hadn't suddenly become tolerable, and he didn't feel any better about the mistake he'd made or what he planned to do to correct it.

Letting out a heavy sigh, Kyle just made his way to the door, deciding to start his shift early rather than kill another twenty minutes standing around Wes.

"GOOD MORNING, MR. MAYNARD. MY NAME'S DOCTOR MONROE and I'm going to be taking care of you today."

Kyle froze in the middle of quieting the monitor. Of course Wes was the doctor on this case. Hidden Creek Memorial was a small hospital, but there were still three other doctors to go around, and so far Kyle's patients had all been assigned to them, not Wes. So much for thinking he had a full day of dodging that bullet.

"I told you I don't wanna hear that racket," Mr. Maynard barked, reminding Kyle of his task.

A middle-aged woman rose from the chair in the corner. "Dad, he's working on it. Please be patient."

The woman—Mary, Eli Maynard's daughter—gave Kyle an apologetic look as he turned off the monitors. It wasn't the first time, and Kyle treated it like all the last. He just gave her a reassuring smile in return and she stopped fidgeting.

"Is that any better, Eli?" Kyle asked.

The room was mostly quiet now, except for the soft beeping of more crucial monitors he wasn't willing to turn off.

"Seeing as how I can hear myself think now, yeah," the man grumbled.

Wes observed these interactions, seeming unconcerned with the fact that his appearance had been all but ignored. Deciding to again take the high road—and prove he wasn't going to back down on this case—Kyle filled the man in.

"This is Eli Maynard and his daughter, Mary." Kyle turned to the woman and smiled encouragingly. "Mary, why don't you tell Dr. Monroe what you told me."

She looked up at Wes, who seemed to sense the high amount of tension in the room. He pulled up a chair on the opposite side of Eli's bed, and Mary visibly relaxed.

"My father was diagnosed with Alzheimer's five years ago. It's late-stage now, and he's..." She looked at her father, and the mix of pain and fatigue in her eyes broke Kyle's heart. "He's a handful. He's become combative, which I was told could happen, but he was always such a sweet man." Her voice shook slightly, but she steeled herself. "Lately I've had trouble getting him to eat and drink as much as he should. He started getting dehydrated, so..."

She gave a helpless shrug, and Kyle offered her a smile for going through all of that again. Even as Eli talked through some of it, raising Cain about being treated like an invalid.

"It looks like he's already been hooked up to IV fluids, and that'll get some nutrients in him. I'll schedule a few unobtrusive tests, just to make sure the lack of appetite isn't a symptom of something else, but this is fairly standard."

Mary nodded, and Kyle fought back the urge to glower at Wes. Of course she knew it was standard. She knew everything about her father's disease. She was his primary caretaker.

"In the meantime, Mary, I have to ask..." Here it came. The concerned question about whether or not she'd considered putting her father into a home. "Do you have any kind of support system? Friends, family, spouse? Anyone who can take care of your needs while you take care of your father's?"

Well, that... wasn't what he'd expected. Kyle stood there, blinking dumbly. Maybe it was a roundabout way of suggesting it. But as Mary explained her situation, Wes just listened attentively. He didn't offer heavy-handed suggestions or unwanted concerns, nor did he interject.

In fact, Eli was the one who finally broke the conversation. "Oh, Stephen. Thank God. Will you tell these people I'll eat when I damn well feel like eating?"

The man looked right at Wes, and it wasn't hard to figure out what was going on. Quietly, Mary clarified.

"Stephen was my other dad. Eli's husband."

"Where were you last night?" Eli pressed. "I missed you. You know I can't sleep when you're not around."

Kyle watched, his whole-body tense as he waited for Wes to burst Eli's illusion. Some doctors seemed to think it was the "kind" thing to do; that it might help a patient reach lucidity faster. In circumstances like this, though, it just seemed excessively cruel to Kyle.

And apparently to Wes, because he smiled at the older man and... reached for his hand. "I'm here now."

Eli's whole expression brightened, and something clenched just behind Kyle's breastbone.

"Last night I had a dream that you were gone. That you were

taken from me," Eli said, his voice desperate. His whole being was fixed on the man he thought was his husband, and he didn't see Mary's sorrow-filled face.

"I'm right here, Eli. But I need you to take care of yourself, okay? And I need you to let Mary help you when I can't be around."

Eli scoffed at this, but when he opened his eyes again, they'd turned misty with unshed tears. "She's just a little girl, Stephen. I don't wanna put her through that..."

"Dad," Mary called, reaching out to rest a tentative hand on his arm.

Eli turned to look at his daughter, his eyes seeming almost apologetic. "You're just a little girl. You shouldn't have to do this."

Kyle had no idea if it was a moment of clarity or if he was just expressing a sentiment he'd felt throughout his life. Either way, he felt tears sting at his own eyes, and he busied himself with updating the order for Eli's IV fluids.

"She's tough, Eli," Wes said, drawing the man's attention. "You raised her to be that way. Stop being so stubborn and let her help." A soft smile touched his lips—the kind that made Kyle's heart do an odd little flip. "For me. Please."

Eli held his head proudly, staring down the man he believed to be his spouse. But finally he let out a sigh, following it with a gravelly chuckle.

"Bastard. You know I can't resist that."

Kyle smiled to himself as the visit transitioned yet again. Wes filled Mary in on what he planned to do and gave the order for Kyle to get a full round of labs worked up. As the two of them prepared to leave—Wes to move on to the next patient, and Kyle to get that order put in immediately—Mary stopped them just outside the curtain.

"I just wanted to thank you," she said, the earnestness in her voice causing a swell of emotion to rise in Kyle again. "Both of you. No one understands what he needs. That's why I can't bring myself to take him anywhere. But you both get it, and you treated him—and me—with respect, so thank you."

"Respect is the bare minimum you're both owed," Wes said, missing the point. Kyle shot him a look, and he added, "And it's the least we can do."

"Dr. Monroe is right. You need a support system as much as Eli does," Kyle said.

Wes nodded. "I'd like to recommend you to a therapist I know personally. She doesn't push, and she has extended hours to accommodate people who are in your situation."

He pulled a pen and a small pad of paper out of the breast pocket of his lab coat. As Kyle watched, he saw Wes take extra care with his handwriting.

"I'd love to talk to someone, but there's no way I can leave him alone that long," she said, looking back at the curtain.

"Maybe you can find someone who does Skype sessions?" Kyle suggested. "There's a website that lists the therapists who do them. May I?"

He gestured to Wes, and the doctor handed over the pen and paper without comment. Kyle wrote the URL of the database he'd found when searching for his own therapist some time ago, then handed both pen and pad back to Wes. Fingers brushed so briefly that if it wasn't for the electricity that arced through his body, Kyle wouldn't have even known it happened.

As it was, he found himself very, very aware of it. Especially when those grey eyes locked with his.

This was the Wes he remembered. This was the man who'd shown him kindness and compassion the night they first met. And this Wes was far more dangerous to him than the man who completely disregarded his input and treated him like a child.

Tearing his gaze away, Wes pulled off the top sheet and handed it to Mary. "I put my cell number on there, as well. Just in case you ever need someone to talk to."

"I don't know what to say..." Mary looked down at the piece of paper, tears in her eyes.

Wes reached out and put a hand on her shoulder, giving it a gentle squeeze. Kyle was almost concerned she might throw herself against the man and start sobbing—he probably would have, were he in her shoes—but she just sniffled, her eyes and nose red as she pulled herself back into the working state she had to maintain to take care of her father.

"I won't forget this," she said softly, looking at Wes and Kyle in turn. "Thank you."

The two men waited as Mary went to be with her father. Kyle assumed Wes was just going to head off to his next patient, but the man stayed put, looking at him in a way that felt... strange. Not bad, necessarily. Just strange.

It almost felt like Wes was seeing something he hadn't before, and he was stuck staring in awe.

"I'll... get those orders in," Kyle said, feeling like a bashful teenager again.

"Good," was Wes' eventual answer, accompanied by a nod, and the word being repeated two more times. Neither of them moved, and finally Wes said, "Come find me when you take your lunch."

And that was that. No explanation, no insight into what that meant before Wes turned and walked away, leaving Kyle to stand there feeling like an idiot. An idiot whose heart was pounding at the idea of a private meeting with Dr. Monroe.

10

WES

*H*e'd wanted to apologize.

He'd intended to do it in the break room, even. Kyle had obviously made an effort, and it was only fair to let the other man know he wasn't solely to blame. They'd both behaved poorly, and the patient suffered because of it.

But he'd been afraid of what he might say and the ways in which his temper might get the better of him, so he'd kept quiet. Somehow he'd managed to avoid Kyle for most of the morning, but when he checked in on Mr. Maynard, he fully expected a repeat of what happened with Mrs. Hartford—despite Kyle's apology.

It had him on edge until Kyle was kind, accommodating, and respectful to the combative man. Playing the role of Stephen had seemed natural—he'd done the same thing for his mother before she passed—and yet he'd expected criticism from Kyle. Many of his colleagues believed playing into the altered state of consciousness was the same as promoting it; even discouraging lucidity.

Kyle said nothing of the sort, and the glances sent his way

suggested the man was impressed and even pleased by Wes' actions. It shouldn't have mattered to him in the slightest, but for some reason, it did.

Then, of course, there was the matter of Mary thanking them. They'd been of equal help to the patient and his daughter, and she'd helped him see that. So too had Kyle, when he suggested a more practical solution to Mary's inability to travel for therapy. It was something she desperately needed, and Kyle seemed to understand that on a sympathetic level.

So he'd asked the man to lunch. Not in so many words, but enough that he could find the rest later. And when Kyle finally sought him out a little after one, he tried to better explain himself.

"I was hoping I could buy you lunch. The cafeteria here is... tolerable," he said with a small twitch of his lips, "but we can go to Rocket if you'd rather."

Kyle blinked up at him in that innocent, adorable way that stirred a hunger within Wes—the same hunger he'd buried after that first day of working alongside the man.

Mostly buried, he reminded himself. It was possible he'd thought of that night, and what might have happened, had Kyle not been too overwhelmed to continue.

"Uh... yeah, no. No, the cafeteria is fine. Lead the way," the man said, gesturing awkwardly.

Wes smirked but did just that, leading Kyle to a place he was sure the man had been multiple times already. Even the staff who didn't eat meals in the cafeteria ended up there to check on orders for patients or to find a colleague who was hiding out.

The cafeteria itself was fairly empty. Most of the lunch orders had already been sent on their way, and the few doctors and nurses that sat at the tables had their attention fixed firmly on their phones.

"I know this is an impressive bounty," he said as they made it up to the front, "but don't bother skimping. Get whatever you like."

That ended up being a roast beef sandwich on whole grain bread, a Caesar salad, a small dish of fruit, and a plain yogurt. Rather tame, as far as the cafeteria was concerned. Wes ordered an open-faced turkey sandwich, fries, and the same dish of fruit—along with a Cherry Coke to help keep him on his feet for the rest of the day.

"Aren't you supposed to be a doctor?" Kyle asked, skeptical of his choices.

Instead of getting agitated by the fact that the man was questioning the nutritional value of his meal—of which there was basically none—Wes just smirked.

"That's what it says on my coat," he jerked his chin down toward his badge.

Kyle looked at him like he'd lost his mind, then burst out laughing. A private smile touched Wes' lips, one he managed to tuck into a believable enough smirk as he paid for their meals and picked out a table.

"You didn't have to do this," Kyle asserted, freeing his sandwich from its plastic wrap prison.

"Maybe. But it gives me a chance to apologize."

The younger man had taken a bite of his sandwich, lettuce and tomato and bread sticking out of his mouth as he stared at Wes once again. Had he really been that much of an ass that something so simple as an apology was unbelievable?

Yes. Yes, he had.

"We both failed Mrs. Hartford," he admitted. "I should have taken more care with the order and made sure you were aware of her history from the old files."

"You mean the files crammed into storage that haven't been digitized or added to the current files in any way?" Kyle asked.

"Those are the ones." Wes unwrapped his silverware packet, preparing to make inroads on his turkey sandwich. "This hospital's systems are..."

"Ancient?" Kyle prompted.

"Prehistoric, is what I was going to say," Wes snorted, "but ancient works too. Either way, that's not your fault and I apologize for taking it out on you."

The man sitting across from him carefully chewed and swallowed his sandwich, watching Wes the whole while as though he expected a sudden change of heart. When Wes just lifted his brows in question, he finally spoke.

"Apology accepted."

Wes nodded and the two of them enjoyed their lunch in somewhat-awkward silence for a time. Both checked their phones—mostly to have something to do—and neither seemed inclined to do anything that might upset this budding truce.

There was so much tension that Wes almost physically cringed when Kyle broke the silence.

"Is... everything okay?"

He looked up from his lunch to find Kyle eyeing him with the same concern he'd shown to patients.

"You just seem like you haven't been sleeping well," he clarified.

It was on the tip of his tongue to fire back that he'd worked thirty-six hour shifts back to back during his residency and no one needed to fuss over him then. But he stopped that knee-jerk reaction, his brow creasing as he considered.

He hadn't been sleeping, even though he had ample time to do so. Normally his bouts of insomnia were caused by a myriad of reasons—most of them centering around memories of Adrian—but this time there was a clearly defined reason.

In that moment, looking at the man who sat across from him, Wes made a choice. He'd offered an apology, yes, but Kyle deserved an explanation, as well.

"The day I told Sloane about our previous encounter," he said, feeling an odd twinge at having to call it that, "he kindly informed me he'd decided to close the hospital."

"What?!"

Kyle's reaction was immediate, his plastic tray clattering as his silverware dropped against it. Wes shot the man a glare as the few people in the cafeteria turned to see what all the fuss was about.

"Please, say that a little louder. I don't think everyone in Hidden Creek heard you."

"Okay, you don't get to snark at me," Kyle protested, glaring at Wes. "I'm not the one who decided to spill the beans in the hospital that's apparently closing."

He had a point there. Wes considered their respective trays, glancing out the window. It was a nice day outside. A little too hot, probably, but at least the likelihood of the sky opening up seemed small right now. Getting ahold of his own tray, Wes pushed out his chair and indicated Kyle's food with his chin. "Grab your tray and follow me."

Kyle gave him a wide-eyed look, his gaze darting around as

though he were the world's worst spy. At any other time, Wes might have found it adorable. Though, who was he kidding. It was still plenty adorable.

"Are we allowed to do that?" he asked in hushed tones.

Wes looked pointedly at the bored cafeteria workers who were serving pre-cooked, pre-packaged meals to staff and visitors alike. Brow lifting, he looked back at Kyle and smirked. "I don't know. There's a very real chance the cafeteria police might bust us."

Kyle rolled his eyes, though there was an amused smile still on his lips. "Is your sarcasm all you have? Because I'm beginning to wonder why anyone fears you."

He kept himself from answering that, not wanting to be drawn back to a dark place. He knew very well why the rest of the staff was intimidated by him; why some even feared him. He'd cultivated an attitude and a way of dealing with things that protected him and his patients, and sometimes—often times—that meant deliberately pissing off the nurses and hospital workers.

Instead, Wes just shouldered the door open, holding his arm above Kyle's head as the shorter man slipped through. The side door of the cafeteria let out to the parking lot, and specifically a part of it that rose in a small incline. It was a bit of a hike to get up the hill, but once they did, that section of the lot was separated from the road—and the other available parking spaces—by one large, rectangular-shaped planter. The planter was made of brick, and the smell of damp soil and mulch reached Wes as he set his tray down, getting the toe of his shoe wedged into the brick to help hoist himself atop it.

After a long moment of skepticism, Kyle did the same, and the men sat side by side, trays in their laps. As Wes had guessed, the midday sun was a harsh observer in their little meeting, and the oak trees rooted in the planter only helped so much.

"So why is Sloane closing the hospital?" Kyle asked, squinting against the sun as he speared a piece of fruit.

"Money." Wes' tone wasn't as laced with bitterness as he thought it might be. What was there to be bitter about? It cost an exorbitant amount of money to keep a hospital running, and Tom only got so many stipends and grants. "Most of the cases that come through our doors are emergent, and there are a fair number of residents in Hidden Creek who have limited insurance—or no insurance at all."

Kyle nodded in understanding. "So the hospital foots the cost of equipment and procedures, with no way to recuperate the loss." The man's brow furrowed as he ate a slice of watermelon. "I never thought one person would be in charge of that."

"Sloane has a financial advisor, and as far as I know he talks to the county at least once a month to request help with the things we can't cover. But the hospital still doesn't bring in any money, and he wants to retire, apparently."

"That doesn't make any sense," Kyle mused. "Why would he hire a new nurse if he knows he's going to close the hospital?"

That was a very good question, and Wes didn't have an answer for the man. "I don't know. I'm guessing there must be more going on that he hasn't told me about. A dispute with the county, maybe pressure to turn this place into a regionalized urgent care facility."

Kyle audibly groaned, returning his fork to his plate as though he were disgusted with the whole thing. "Those facilities help supplement an existing hospital. They aren't a replacement for it."

There was no need for Wes to say anything. They both knew that to be the truth, and yet it changed nothing. Sloane had made up his mind. Hard facts and statistics weren't going to convince him to dig himself deeper into debt. Wes had to find another way—

something that would work whether Sloane's conscience won out or not.

"I'm guessing that's why you look like you've been working back-to-back, twenty-four-hour shifts," Kyle mused.

Wes finally cracked open his soda, letting some of the carbonation settle before he took a drink. Bubbles tickled his nose, dampening his upper lip as he drank, but he hardly cared. The taste of cold cherry soda on a hot day was transportive. He was a kid again, sitting on the docks with his friends, packing as much into his summer vacation as he could before school started back up.

Caught up in nostalgia—in a time before he'd had to worry about anyone but himself—it took Wes a long moment to confirm. He finally did with a nod, and Kyle let out a sigh beside him. When he looked over at the man, mossy green eyes were sizing him up. Not with lust or agitation this time, but with an appraising look that suggested Kyle was still trying to figure out what to make of him.

"This hospital means a lot to you, doesn't it," he said softly.

Wes looked out over the myriad of parked cars and trucks, squinting through the glare of the sun. Hidden Creek Memorial wasn't anything special as far as buildings were concerned. It was built out of concrete—to weather even the most brutal storms—though the county had pitched in for a brick facade when he was a boy. The bricks were chipped and sun-worn now, some of them having fallen away. So many of them had become damaged or otherwise unwieldy on the south side that Hidden Creek High participated in a project to strip it back to the concrete and paint a mural there when Wes was a junior. Every four years, the mural was retouched, and more students added to it. The last time was two years ago, and some very talented—and mischievous—kid had painted a picture of Batman and Robin of all things, in a white doctor's coat and nurse's scrubs respectively, with a rainbow-colored Batmobile in the background.

To this day he still had no idea what the story was behind that addition, but it had become the face of Hidden Creek Memorial, along with a potpourri of animals, people, and landscape elements.

"This hospital is everything to me," Wes said, finally returning his gaze to Kyle.

Their eyes held, locked for several long moments. The man sitting next to him looked so painfully earnest, as though he felt Wes' pain himself. Maybe it was just that he had something to lose in this, too. Something more practical. That had to be it, and Wes shored up his defenses, addressing that particular elephant as he went back to his sandwich.

"Sloane will find placements for everyone, if that's what you're worried about. If the hospital is turned into a clinic, I'm sure they'll have space for you. If not, you'll get a glowing letter of recommendation for a position of your choice. I know how all of this seems, but Tom Sloane is a good man."

A good man who'd been stretched to his breaking point. It happened, and Wes had to remind himself of that all too often as he thought of those doors closing—of that mural chipping and fading away.

"That's not what I'm worried about," Kyle said, a hint of annoyance in his voice. "I mean, yeah. Part of the reason I came here was because I had a job lined up, but I can figure something else out. I have a working car and the ability to move my schedule around. Not all of our patients have that. What the hell are they supposed to do if they have more than a head cold?"

Kyle's sudden burst of passion was like a beacon, drawing Wes in.

It was quite possibly one of the worst times to think about—and fixate on—the man's lips, but something in Wes came alive at this display. He was used to the people around him just treating this like any other job. To see someone who actually understood the problem and empathized with those involved... it was a strange turn-on to have, but he wasn't going to deny it.

"Find transportation to a crowded regional hospital, apparently. And most of those are an hour away." Pulling the napkin out of his silverware packet, Wes dabbed at his mouth.

Kyle, meanwhile, looked at his own tray in what Wes would describe as self-righteous disgust. After a beat, he set it aside. "Why are you telling me this?" he finally asked.

Why *was* he telling Kyle? It wasn't that he wanted someone to join him in his mix of fury and misery, though it was nice to have company for once. He wasn't exactly sure, and all he said was, "I thought you deserved to know. But I'm taking care of it. I have a few ideas that might buy us some time; keep this place open."

Kyle turned to look at him dubiously, and in doing so, the man's thigh brushed Wes'. Heat arced through his body and his whole being suddenly became very aware of the other man's closeness. "Okay, I say this with the utmost respect, from the bottom of my heart: You look like shit. Handling all of this on your own? It's not working for you."

Wes' lips curved in amusement, an action that finally seemed to draw Kyle's attention. The man's gaze moved to his mouth, and Wes felt the shift when he, too, realized they were sitting close. "So you're saying if I'd looked like this the night we met, you wouldn't have gone home with me?"

He couldn't help it. Maybe it was hormones stirred up by stress. Maybe it was just the opportunity for distraction. Whatever it was, Wes had decided to abandon decorum—and apparently risk fucking up whatever progress he and Kyle had made—all for the opportunity to tease the man. And oh, was it worth it. Kyle's pale cheeks flooded scarlet, and he made a concerted effort not to look away. It was like a rabbit facing down a panther, and Wes had the worst thoughts about making a "meal" of this man.

"Probably not," Kyle said, though his body language told another story.

His eyes were on Wes' lips, his muscles stiff with tension, but leaning ever so slightly toward him. It was insane to have this moment outside of a hospital, during a shift, when they'd just been discussing the hospital closing. But here they were, having come full circle, and it was all Wes could do to make coherent words come out of his mouth.

"I guess I'll have to let you help me, then. So I don't keep looking like shit." The corner of his lips hooked upward slowly. "Wouldn't want to upset the patients."

"That's how you're asking for my help?" Kyle asked, a slight tremor in his voice even as he smiled. "By flirting with me?"

Wes gave a slight shrug, as if to say, "guilty." He was, after all. And the fact that Kyle was willing to call him on it just made things that much more interesting. But rather than let the other man respond, he officially confirmed by bridging that last gap and pressing his lips to Kyle's.

It wasn't the frenzied, passionate, forget-about-an-ex kiss they'd shared at his place, and with good reason. They knew each other better now, already well past the moment where Wes should have considered this a good idea.

But the sweetness of Kyle's lips, the softness and acceptance he found as the man slowly returned the sentiment, was like eighty-proof whiskey downed straight from the barrel. It made him forget all of the reasons they shouldn't do this. It made him forget the fact that they were still technically at work and anyone could see them. It made him forget the very reason he'd led Kyle out here in the first place.

The more comfortable Kyle became, the more he leaned into the kiss, every inch of his lips joined with Wes', his tongue seeking entrance Wes easily granted. The kiss deepened and a soft, whimper of a moan caught in Kyle's throat when Wes sucked the man's tongue into his mouth.

That moment, that response, was enough to spook the less experienced man and he broke the kiss, looking up at Wes with glassy, lust-filled eyes that were still half closed. He cleared his throat and looked away, his cheeks burning scarlet.

"I'll help you," he said, his voice strained.

And then—to Wes' amusement—he hopped down from the edge of the planter, grabbed his tray, and headed back to the cafeteria as though nothing happened.

11

WES

$\mathcal{I}$t was rare that Wes ever got someone so stuck in his head that thinking about them interfered with his work. So rare, in fact, that it had never happened. Even with Adrian, he'd kept a strict divide between his personal and professional life. And every man since had been an exercise in escapism —a means to forget about whatever drama was happening at the hospital.

Kyle went against all of that, and he hadn't even fucked the man. The most they'd done was kiss, and while they were some of the most hungry, passionate kisses Wes had ever experienced, it wasn't like he had the promise of more to look forward to. Kyle made it clear that first night that he wasn't ready for more, and considering just how much of a farce their meeting had been the next morning, he doubted the man was going to reconsider any time soon.

So that left him with an attraction he couldn't do anything about, to a man who was painfully available—Wes saw him every day at work, after all—but patently off limits.

Now that they'd mended their professional dispute, Kyle had also become one of the few people who didn't immediately start walking the other way when they saw him. He'd seen several of the man's patients, and grew more at ease with his competence. It wasn't implicit trust—no one had that from him—but it was something, and it made the patient experience better to a noticeable degree.

It also made the other staff talk; especially the nurses. Every time he walked by the nurses' station, conversation immediately stopped. He was used to that, but the same thing now happened to Kyle. It was enough to convince him that they needed to find a discreet place to talk about the hospital closing.

That was why he'd told Kyle to meet him in the on-call room during his lunch break. That, and the fact that he apparently liked testing his own boundaries.

The on-call room at Hidden Creek Memorial was small and... cozy was a nice way of putting it, he supposed, though not completely accurate. There were a few cots in the corners, along with a counter that housed a mini fridge, a toaster oven, and a microwave. It was mostly meant to be used by doctors who were staying at the hospital over long periods of time, giving them a chance to sleep and eat without having to leave the building.

Back when he'd done his residency in North Carolina, they'd had an entire floor of on-call rooms and residents used those with a reasonable guarantee of privacy. Here, the risk was somewhat high of another doctor or a nurse just barging in.

It was a deterrent, at least, and it kept him on his best behavior when Kyle entered about ten minutes after he had. The fact that the man's gaze automatically went to one of the cots—and then to Wes—didn't help matters much, but he just raised a brow and waited for the accusation.

"Is this really the best place to talk?" he asked dubiously.

"With the exception of the roof, it's the most private place in the hospital. And in case you haven't noticed, it's about a million degrees outside today, so I'm not exactly eager to sit out in the sun."

"Yeah. I forgot how humid this part of Texas can get," Kyle grumbled, taking a seat at the small table—the only other feature aside from the beds and appliances.

Kyle pulled out a manila folder and flipped it open, revealing an entire stack of printed sheets that contained numbers all the way down. Wes took a seat opposite the man and examined one of the papers—it looked like some kind of expense report.

"Are these for the hospital?" he asked, sifting through a few of them. At Kyle's nod, he added, "How'd you get a copy of the hospital's finances?"

"A bit of digging through public records. Hidden Creek Memorial is classified as a non-profit, so they have to provide solid accounting to keep that classification."

Impressive. Wes met Kyle's gaze across the table and watched as the man drew in a breath. His pupils dilated, his nostrils flared, and Wes would have sworn the man was thinking about anything other than those numbers.

The knowledge of that power was intoxicating, and Wes was oh so tempted to push the boundaries he'd already told himself he was going to avoid. But considering they were tasked with the most unerotic work in the history of the universe and still Kyle was getting ideas from the close proximity and the presence of many different surfaces, the effort seemed futile.

"I thought we could look for any discrepancies—anywhere the

hospital can cut back without affecting patient care," Kyle said, tearing his gaze away.

"Am I making you nervous?" Amusement edged his voice. He couldn't help it. He hadn't even done anything and Kyle was on edge.

"What? No," he answered, a little too quickly.

Wes bit back a smirk, turning his attention to the papers. As they worked, Kyle handed him a pen. They both underlined discrepancies, going through the divided stack without comment for a while.

Finally, Kyle said, "I don't know why you're playing coy. You know exactly why I'm nervous."

"I thought you weren't," Wes lobbed back, one brow arching playfully.

Kyle just rolled his eyes. "Maybe you make a habit of kissing people you work with, but I don't," he asserted. "Now you tell me to come to the on-call room with you. Alone. Surrounded by beds. What am I supposed to think?"

Wes took a moment to digest all of that in his mind. First, Kyle's tone. He sounded annoyed, but only mildly so. It wasn't an accusation, he noted, just an observation.

Then he took note of the fact that Kyle somehow thought he—the man who got along with precisely one of his co-workers—had these kinds of encounters all the time. While it was true he wasn't picky in the past, everything he did stayed out of the hospital.

The fact that Kyle tempted him to break that unspoken rule—was tempting him even now, in fact, with that pouty, self-righteous look—was troublesome. And exciting.

There was also the fact that Kyle was obviously distracted, and that was what Wes chose to focus on.

"What are you thinking now, exactly?" He rose slowly from his chair, as if fearing Kyle might bolt if he made any sudden movements.

"Right now?" Kyle's Adam's apple bobbed as he looked up at Wes. "I'm thinking about the fact that you probably planned this."

"I didn't." No sense hiding it. No sense pretending he was a saint, either. "But I'm not going to turn down an opportunity, either."

Kyle's breath hitched, his eyes wide, pupils fully dilated as he focused on Wes—or more specifically, on his lips. He hadn't planned on this happening. He'd told himself he was going to behave. But Kyle was practically taunting him at this point. Throwing out the bait and seeing if Wes took it.

Normally he liked to see his partners give in. He liked to conserve his own willpower solely to watch other people beg. But Kyle Harris did something to him; something Wes still couldn't describe.

All he knew was that if he could have another taste, he wasn't going to let the moment pass him by.

Stopping in front of Kyle's chair, he nudged the man's knees apart with his own, insinuating himself even closer. Warm hands moved over the breadth of Kyle's shoulders, sliding inward as his fingers curled around the collar of the man's scrubs.

Through it all, Kyle remained defiant—but not stoic. His breathing was irregular, he looked up at Wes with pure heat in his gaze, and his lower lip trembled with the effort to keep from giving in.

"Why even agree to meet me here, if you thought this was an

option?" Wes asked, leaning down so the warmth of his breath teased Kyle's skin as he spoke.

The younger man tried to suppress a full-body shudder and failed. "I—"

"Admit it. You wanted this to happen."

Kyle swallowed thickly, but lifted his chin that much more. "I'm not admitting anything."

Wes' lips curved into a sly smile, his gaze fixed on Kyle's mouth. The man's lips were just barely parted, and Wes used the leverage he had to pull Kyle slowly to his feet, his fingers gripping the neckline of the man's scrubs.

Kyle came willingly, letting out a puff of hot breath as the two of them were suddenly face to face, inches away from each other. Wes' whole body was wound more tightly than he'd ever experienced before. His cock ached, and they hadn't even done anything yet. He just wanted the man before him so much that his imagination was able to fill in a vividly enticing picture of what they could be doing.

"If you don't want this, then I guess I'll go back to staring at expense reports..." he taunted, running the tip of his tongue over Kyle's still-trembling bottom lip.

That earned a gasp, and one that sent a thrill rushing through him. Wes made the most of that moment, hoping to prove his point as his hands moved down to Kyle's ass. The loose scrub pants weren't doing him any favors, but he was able to get a handful of the other man's cheeks, and he used that grip to pull Kyle toward him, letting the man feel just how hard he was.

The second, shuddering gasp was confirmation enough, and Wes was ready to move in for the kill. It didn't matter if he was the one who caved first. He wanted Kyle. Badly. And it was obvious Kyle wanted him, too. Even knowing he'd only get a taste, Wes was more than willing to indulge.

But before his mouth could claim Kyle's, the shrill beep of his pager sent an annoyingly unsexy vibration through him. He grimaced, still a hair's breadth away from the other man, able to feel Kyle's breath on his lips. It was probably nothing. It could probably wait. But the longer Wes let himself think that, the guiltier he felt.

Finally he stepped back from Kyle and reached for his pager. "There's a trauma coming in."

Kyle sobered quickly, reaching past Wes to grab the papers and stuff them back into the folder. "We can go over these later. Somewhere that's..." he let out an exasperated huff. "Somewhere that's not here."

Despite the urgency, Wes still found himself wanting to indulge in that kiss. Especially when he caught the look of longing in Kyle's moss green eyes. But he straightened his coat, banished the thoughts from his mind, and went to do his job.

KYLE

*K*yle sat on his new couch, one leg curled up on the cushion in front of him, trying desperately to focus on the expense reports in his lap and not the memory of Wes' hard body pressing against his.

He wasn't an accountant. He'd enjoyed math and science in school, but he didn't find numbers particularly thrilling. They were just straightforward; easy to understand. Governed by simple rules. Unlike his attraction to a certain doctor.

He shifted again, letting out a huff. So far he'd been looking at the same sheet for... almost a half hour, according to the clock on the DVR. That wasn't going to cut it. Not when they needed to find an answer to this mess as quickly as possible. The MVA—motor vehicle accident—that came in had tied both of them up for a while, and things stayed hectic all through Kyle's shift, at least. He only saw glimpses of Wes, and the man looked harried and preoccupied as he hurried off from patient to patient.

He'd considered looking for Wes after his shift ended—or rather, after he left the hospital, since he didn't get around to doing that until two hours later—but that seemed like a terrible idea. Being alone with him at work was bad enough. Wes might suggest they go back to his apartment or to Kyle's house to look at the numbers, and he might agree to it.

Because some devilish part of him wanted to be caught out. He wanted to give Wes an excuse to act on the attraction that burned between them.

Letting out an annoyed groan, Kyle shifted again and held the papers up to the lamp. They were easy enough to read in a more relaxed position, but he hoped staring at the words and numbers would keep his thoughts from straying to Wes.

And for a little while, it worked. He was able to mark some areas where the hospital might be able to cut back. The cafeteria got a lot of its produce from a regional distributor. If they started buying from the local farms—the Meile farms, if he remembered right—they could get fresher food at a better price. The mark-up on meals seemed a little low, too. There was no way the staff and community wouldn't agree to paying a little bit more for their food if it meant the doors stayed open. And then there were maintenance and utility costs for rooms that were barely used, product deals that could be renegotiated, insurance rates that needed to be looked at by a professional...

It was progress, and Kyle was pleased with himself as he put together a list of things to speak with Wes about. The moment he thought of just how and where they'd do that, though, his mind fixated full force on that on-call room again.

On-call rooms weren't a necessary expenditure, right? They could have that thing repurposed or demolished tomorrow and everything would be fine. The doctors could nap in the break room, where it was much more likely for someone to come strolling in and interrupt things that definitely weren't napping.

Yes, that sounded like a perfectly reasonable solution to his inability to control himself around Wes Monroe. So reasonable that he spent another half hour thinking about sliding his hands under Wes' coat in the break room; undoing the man's slacks just enough to...

"Fuck," Kyle growled. "What is wrong with you?"

This seemed worse than run of the mill horniness. That he could usually alleviate by beating off. But then... he hadn't exactly tried to do that in this case, had he? He'd never jacked off to thoughts of another man before, and somehow it didn't cross his mind that doing so might give him enough blood flow back to his brain and away from his needy cock.

He'd already made peace with the attraction. This was just the next step. Like when he'd first discovered what to do with all those pent-up hormones in junior high. He'd made his teenage years a lot easier on himself by giving his right hand a thorough workout, and he was confident release would be just what he needed again.

So he set the papers well away from himself and went to fetch a hand towel and some lube from his bedroom. Normally he would have grabbed his tablet, too, but some stubborn part of him wanted to see just what he could create in his mind, without the conscious aid of porn.

It wasn't like he lacked fantasies, after all. The same one kept playing through his mind, over and over.

Getting comfortable on the couch, Kyle set the lube and towel beside him and just focused on the easier, less messy stimulation first. He relaxed his body, stretching out so his ankles were hanging over the opposite arm of the couch, his hand resting on his stomach before he slowly moved it down.

He thought of Wes doing the same, the way he had in the on-call room. Large, warm hands moving over his body, lighting up every nerve ending even through his scrubs. The first time, he'd just gripped Kyle's collar, but it was easy for his imagination to alter that path. He pictured the other man's hand moving down to his hip, then his thigh. He lingered there for a moment before moving inward, and Kyle squeezed his cock through his sweatpants, a soft moan falling from his lips.

He was already half hard, and he hadn't even done anything yet. Needing that to change, Kyle gave himself another squeeze, then moved to cup his balls. Wes seemed like the kind of man who knew exactly what he was doing, and there was no doubt in Kyle's mind that the other man would attend to those oft-neglected areas.

He rubbed himself through his pants, thinking of Wes doing the same. Neither of them would be content with that for long, he thought. They only had so much time in that on-call room before someone came across them. So just as he hooked his thumbs into the waistband of his sweatpants, he imagined Wes doing the same to his scrubs.

From there, it was easy to undo the snap on his boxers and slip his hand through the silky cloth. It was almost shockingly cool against the searing hot flesh that pulsed in his hand, his fingers closing around his dick. Getting a firm grip, he started slowly as he remembered that first night and Wes' hand on him. That had been through his underwear, but it was enough to let him know what kind of grip the man would have. Firm. Confident. He'd move with sure strokes, tugging Kyle's dick like it was his own.

Letting his thighs fall further apart, Kyle reached for the dispenser of lube and squeezed some into his palm. The slick liquid joined the precum that beaded at his slit, and he used both to coat his length until it glistened and his hand glided easily over his flesh.

From there, all bets were off.

As he stroked himself, Kyle didn't just think of Wes' hand working him. He thought of the man's mouth with those soft lips and that expert tongue pressing to every sensitive spot Kyle had ever found on his own—and maybe even some he hadn't. He thought of Wes on his knees, still looking confident and completely in control as he took Kyle's cock to the root, not stopping until his lips touched the man's pelvis.

"Oh, fuck," he moaned, his hand working faster over his aching dick.

That was when the fantasy changed. This time, it wasn't Wes on his knees—it was Kyle. He was braced before Wes' slim hips, his nails raking over the V that cut a perfect path down to the man's cock.

Kyle had never handled another man before, but it was easy to imagine. He'd felt Wes' erection. The doctor seemed a bit bigger than him; thicker. With his eyes closed, he could imagine it easily. His fingers eased their choke hold on his own dick and he stroked in a slow, deliberate pattern, imagining himself looking up into those steel grey eyes.

And while he'd definitely never sucked a man off before, it wasn't long before he was lowering his head in his fantasy and taking the crown of Wes' cock between his lips. He imagined the taste of salt and sweat, and the pulsing warmth against his mouth.

As understanding as Wes had been, Kyle wasn't sure he wanted an understanding partner in this fantasy. He imagined the man's long fingers gripping his hair so close to the scalp that it hurt, then ramming his cock past Kyle's barely-parted lips. Shoving it in as Kyle played at resistance—very much wanting to be handled that way, but acting like the defiant boy he knew Wes responded to.

His own actions became more frantic as he thought of being used —of Wes thrusting hard and deep into his mouth, over and over again. He pumped his leaking cock furiously, his hand moving down to pay much-needed attention to his aching balls. He lifted his ass off the couch to better accommodate the cupping and stroking and tugging, and another image suddenly surged into his conscious mind:

Wes bending him over that table they'd been working at and fucking him so hard the damn thing collapsed under them.

Kyle felt his balls tighten, his release so close. He bit down on his lip, squeezing the base of his cock to try and delay the inevitable. He wasn't ready yet. There was something else he wanted to experience before he came.

Grabbing the lube with his free hand, Kyle fumbled with it, squirting some out and using it to coat one finger. He lifted up even more, draping his legs over the back of the couch, and ran that slick finger along the rim of his asshole, shuddering instantly from the explosion of sensation that followed.

He'd always wanted to try this; to see what it felt like. None of his partners had ever been adventurous enough. With some, he hadn't even felt comfortable bringing it up, and he'd never taken the leap on his own.

Now, though, as he imagined another man pushing his cock past that tight ring of muscle, stretching his inexperienced hole open, it was all too easy for him to slip a finger inside himself. And when that found barely any resistance, a second one.

He pumped at first, moving his fingers in and out, imagining Wes fucking him. And then the pad of his finger touched something inside of him that made him gasp, all the breath suddenly stolen from his lungs.

The hand on his cock stilled as he focused all his energy on that sensation. He pressed against the spongy tissue again, then started stroking it, taking full advantage of the pleasure that arced through him as he made himself more familiar with his own body.

It only took a short amount of stroking before his balls suddenly tightened. He tried to delay the orgasm again, but it overpowered him, the force of it making him press hard against the couch as he rode out the blinding wave of pleasure.

And all the while he imagined Wes on top of him, holding his thighs, pounding into him with expert control. His body clenched around his own fingers, and as he shook and trembled with the strength of his orgasm, he knew one thing with absolute certainty:

Getting off to the thought of Wes Monroe didn't remotely diminish his desire for the real thing. If anything, he wanted it more now, and he knew the next time they were alone together in that on-call room, he wasn't going to be able to stop himself.

13

WES

*H*aving a day off gave Wes a chance to reflect. With the expense reports emailed to him—along with Kyle's notes—he was able to make headway on isolating and writing up the things that could be scaled back or removed entirely with little to no impact on the patients. Some of the ideas weren't going to make him especially popular with the staff, but he already wasn't well liked. No sense walking on eggshells. Either people compromised, or everyone lost their jobs.

By the time he walked into the hospital to start his next shift, he'd prepared something to discuss with Kyle. He had no doubt they were going to butt heads, but he had ways of being persuasive. Even if those ways typically involved ample distraction, which Wes told himself he was not going to engage in this time.

It'd been bad enough the day before. Had his pager not interrupted, Wes might well have had Kyle's scrub pants around his ankles before too much longer. He'd been thinking with his dick to the exclusion of all else; taking risks that were usually beneath him. For all that he got around, he'd never fucked anyone at work.

And yet if Kyle gave him the opportunity, he wasn't sure he had the willpower to turn it down. No matter what he told himself.

Fortunately, Wes greeted the day content with the knowledge that Kyle had likely spent that time regretting his actions. The man might attempt to lay down some ground rules, and for his own sanity and self-preservation, Wes would be inclined to follow them. There was still a chance something might happen outside of work, and it was oh so tempting to suggest they formulate a plan at Bottom's Up or, better yet, his apartment.

But for now, he went into work ready to focus on his patients. Cora was scheduled for a post-op today, and Wes devoted his thoughts to her and everyone else he needed to take care of.

Once Wes' part was done, he stepped out of the room only to be followed by Kyle, who appeared a few moments after him. Wes finished writing down his last observations and notes and clicked the pen away, sliding it into the pocket of his coat.

"Did you need me to authorize anything else?" he asked, wondering if he'd forgotten something.

It seemed unlikely. He'd been thorough, and his mind had only drifted to Kyle—and how much of a tragedy it was, again, for that tight ass of his to be hidden in formless scrub pants—one time.

But apparently this wasn't about some oversight. "No, every-thing's taken care of. I just thought we could meet up later. Same Bat-time, same Bat-place."

Wes' mouth tilted into a smirk. Kyle was nervous for some reason, and he was expressing it by being a bit of a dork. It was an endearing quality, and Wes found himself wanting to kiss and lick the path of red that traveled up the man's neck as he blushed.

"On-call room? Or did you have some other Batcave in mind?" he asked.

"On-call room," Kyle murmured, and it seemed to take the man added effort to meet Wes' gaze. "I'll be off in about an hour."

As the nurse's eyes finally lifted to his own, Wes swore he saw a flash of heat. That was probably just his imagination, though, and his lustful mind seeing what he wanted to see.

Obviously Kyle wasn't calling him to the on-call room to do anything more than discuss the hospital.

But as that hour dragged on, he felt the nerves coil in his gut. His body thrummed with anticipation, and every muscle tightened like an overwrought spring. Images played through his mind, fantasies not unlike the ones that kept creeping in over the past few days.

He took a detour before heading to the on-call room, spending a few moments in the men's room to collect himself and splash some cold water on his face. One look at himself in the mirror was enough to shame most of those thoughts away; at least enough to remind him he wasn't a horny teenager anymore.

When he stepped into the on-call room, though, Kyle was already there and waiting. Not with a stack of papers or a laptop, but with a fire in his eyes that shot right through Wes. Reaching behind him, Wes locked the door, and every thread of anticipation he'd tried to sever wound tight through him again.

"We can't keep doing this," Kyle insisted, his voice ragged. "I can't keep wanting to jump you every time I see you."

That hunger flared to life, but still he kept it at bay. It took every shred of willpower he had, yet he managed. If Kyle wanted anything from him, he was going to have to ask for it or make a move himself.

That didn't keep him from toying with the man, however. "There's an easy solution to that."

"I know." Pulling off his ID and stethoscope, Kyle set them on a nearby table. He went for the hem of his scrub top, and Wes' brow rose to his hairline. "We get it out of our systems."

Get it out of their systems. That sounded surprisingly reasonable and very in-line with Wes' own thinking. He took a step forward, closing the gap between them, but still he didn't act.

"No more games, then." Wes' voice lowered, taking on a rumbling cadence. "You need to tell me exactly what you want."

Stripping off his scrub top to reveal a white undershirt beneath, Kyle said, "I'd rather just show you."

He had no idea which of them moved first. At this point, it didn't matter. Kyle's hands were behind his neck, fingers buried in his hair, and Wes had a grip on the other man's ass. They crashed together, bodies and mouths meeting, tongues colliding in a desperate bid to get closer.

Kyle wasted no time, hands moving to Wes' coat. He gripped the collar and yanked it back over Wes' shoulders. Wes held out his arms to accommodate the motion, feeling frantic as his eyes locked with Kyle's. Once the coat was discarded, his hands gripped the other man's shoulders and he kissed him fiercely, desperately, forcing Kyle back toward one of the cots.

Metal clanged and scraped, and by the time he'd pushed the younger man down, Kyle had pulled up the bottom of Wes' shirt and hooked his fingers into his belt, bringing him down into the cramped space.

There was barely enough room for him to brace atop the man, but Wes hardly noticed. He held himself up with his forearms and kept kissing Kyle, letting out a moan when the man pinned underneath him lifted his ass off the thin mattress and wrapped his legs around Wes, bringing them into closer contact. That taste of friction triggered something primal in him, and he started to pump his hips, grinding against the man despite the fact that they were both still far too clothed below the waist. As worked up as he was, it almost didn't matter, and Kyle seemed to be in the same state. He pitched his head back and moaned, prompting Wes to clap a hand over his mouth to quiet him.

Taking advantage of the power he had, Wes dragged his lips over Kyle's throat, moving down to the collar of his shirt. One hand slid down to the hem and pushed it up, revealing warm, bare skin that was lightly dusted with hair.

The cot creaked beneath their combined weight as Wes shifted, his shoes on the floor. Kyle's scrub pants were easy to untie and tug down, and the man graciously lifted up to help get them off, revealing an impressive bulge.

Normally Wes would have teased, but his mind was switched into frenzy mode, desire pulsing through his veins and filling him with the need to have this man in any and every way he could. Right now, that meant mouthing him through the thin fabric of his boxers, pressing his lips tight around the hard ridge of his erection. Kyle's moan seeped out from between Wes' fingers and Wes grew more vigilant, making sure his palm covered the other man's mouth even as Kyle sat up to watch him.

With his free hand, Wes undid the snap and reached into Kyle's boxers, pulling out his cock. It was scorching hot in his hand, the velvety skin pulled taut over hard, pulsing flesh. He wasted no time, taking the sensitive head between his lips and pushing down, his eyes casting up to Kyle.

Sweat and musk and salt mixed with Wes' own saliva as he sucked greedily, first the head and then a few inches more. One of Kyle's hands fisted in his hair, the other grabbing the metal frame of the cot above him. Wes finally pulled his hand from the other man's mouth, but only because he needed it to tug Kyle's pants—and then his boxers—down the rest of the way until they pooled uselessly around his ankles.

"Fuck," Kyle rasped as Wes took him deeper, lips pressed tightly to the man's shaft, his cock glistening with saliva.

He moved up and down, his tongue pressing to the sensitive bit of flesh just beneath the head. Kyle's grip tightened, the bed frame shaking as he lifted up, his hips rising toward Wes' face. He could tell the man was trying to be quiet, but his expression was twisted in torturous pleasure, his teeth obviously bearing down on his lip.

Wes released him with a loud pop, his hand replacing his mouth as he jerked Kyle's slick cock. "Is this what you wanted?" he asked, his own voice hoarse.

Before the man could answer, he ducked his head down and drew one of Kyle's balls into his mouth, laving over his sac before he worked the other. A muffled moan came from his partner, his hips bucking.

"Do I need to find a way to keep you quiet?" Wes' voice was a deep growl, lust having replaced his common sense.

He felt a twinge of guilt right after, though, remembering just how inexperienced Kyle was. That dominant routine might have been fine with somebody who wanted it, but Kyle was just wading into these waters. Getting his cock sucked by another man who was hungry for it was a completely different level from being fed that same man's cock until he couldn't take anymore.

But Kyle surprised him yet again, a fire sparking in his eyes that was all consuming. He yanked hard at Wes' hair, and Wes lifted his head with a gasp.

118

Whether it was mutual, frenzied lust or something deeper, he felt connected to the man who gripped his shoulders, wordlessly urging him to his feet. He knew instantly what Kyle wanted before he even went for Wes' belt. By the time his fly was down, he was completely on board, one hand gripping the same bed frame Kyle had used to stabilize himself earlier.

Still something in him spoke louder than his all-consuming need. With his free hand he gripped Kyle's chin, tilting his face up so their eyes could meet. A silent question waited in Wes' eyes—an offer for Kyle to back out of this now, no harm done. Something softened in the other man's eyes as he understood, but it was soon replaced by the same burning need that drove him to yank down Wes' pants and underwear in one go.

Wes' cock sprang free, thick and aching for attention. Kyle immediately obliged, wrapping his hand around Wes' length and stroking slowly.

Some of that forceful passion died—Wes could see it in the other man's eyes as they cast up at him. He wasn't lost, exactly, but he was second-guessing himself. Wes thought back to his first time with another man and easily remembered just how nervous he'd been.

He'd gotten through it, yes, but choking on another man's dick had not been the highlight he'd hoped to take away from his first time giving a blowjob. Others might have said it was a rite of passage, but Wes was less inclined to make anyone's first experience a less than amazing one if he could help it.

So he reached down and placed his hand on Kyle's wrist, all while trying to calm the need that surged through him. "You don't have to do this."

"I want to," Kyle said immediately. Then, after a moment, he added, "I'm just... not sure where to start." He let out a short, humorless laugh. "That sounds really, really stupid. I mean, I've got your dick in my hand. It's not that big a mystery. All I have to—"

His finger went to Kyle's lips, stopping him from giving any more of his rambling, self-detrimental apology.

"It's not intuitive," Wes assured him. "Just... think about what you like, and start from there."

"Right. That would require my brain working right now," Kyle muttered.

A smirk touched Wes' lips, but it slowly faded as he realized Kyle was still stuck inside his own insecurities, stroking without much purpose.

"I can guide you?" he asked carefully.

It was a fine line to walk. Wes enjoyed taking the reins; being the dominant one in his sexual encounters. He also enjoyed teaching, and while the two things sometimes went hand in hand, some men considered it a blow to their pride. It was as if they'd been told they should be proficient in what every partner wants before even meeting them, which—in Wes' mind—was ridiculous.

Kyle seemed to have no such hang-ups, though. His eyes widened slightly, that moss green darkening like a forest in the midst of winter, and then he simply nodded.

So Wes began to teach.

"Firmer grip," he said, widening his stance so Kyle had better access. He hissed out a breath when the man's fingers curled more tightly around his cock. "Tight at the base, then ease up as you move upward."

It was what he liked, at least, and when Kyle started to stroke him that way, he felt that desire returning, thrumming hot through his veins. With a couple more instructions, the man gained confidence, and it was easy to tell the moment jacking someone else became almost second nature. He even swiped his thumb over Wes' slit, an action that made him gasp as Kyle used the beaded moisture there to provide a bit of lubrication.

When Kyle's hand settled at the base of his cock and he moved his mouth closer, hot breath playing over the head of his cock, Wes took those questioning eyes of his as a plea for further instruction.

"Start small. Don't try to take more than you're ready for." Kyle hesitated, and Wes moved one hand to the back of his head, gently guiding him until his lips were positioned over the crown of his cock. "Just barely part your lips."

Wes lifted his hips slowly, pressing the head against Kyle's lips. He reveled in even that slight pressure against sensitive flesh, then pushed carefully past the barrier, just slipping the head in. A moan shook through him and he turned his head, stifling it in his arm.

God, why was this doing so much for him? This slow, deliberate learning process was getting him closer to the edge than even the most practiced partners had. Maybe it was the sense of control. Maybe it was the trusting way Kyle looked up at him, or the expressions on his face as he experienced these things for the first time. Whatever it was, Wes wanted more.

"Apply pressure, and use your tongue when you're comfortable," he managed, his voice a little shaky as his hips rocked gently, the head of his cock disappearing into Kyle's mouth, then slowly withdrawing.

Kyle's tongue slipped past his lips and pressed against Wes' slit, his head falling back as he let out a measured breath. "That's it," he encouraged, slowly feeding the man more, inch by inch, until Kyle's lips were stretched around his cock.

His rhythm stayed slow. Steady. Predictable. His hips rolled just enough to bring him closer and then pull away. Kyle opened his mouth wider, taking him in and exploring with his lips and tongue.

"Ready for more?" Wes asked, his fingers curling in Kyle's thick hair, tugging just enough to let him know he was going to take off the training wheels.

Kyle made an enthusiastic sound and nodded as much as he could, and Wes gripped the bed frame with his free hand again, using it as leverage. Rather than go in deeper and force the other man to deep throat before he was ready, he just increased the pace and power of his thrusts, varying them so that they became a little more erratic.

The required instruction became less and less as Kyle got into it. Wes could tell the moment his insecurities disappeared, and he became caught up in the moment just as much as he was earlier. Wes let go of his control as Kyle found his footing, succumbing to the man's lips and tongue as he put into practice everything he'd learned.

When he drew Wes in deeper, the head of his dick nearly reaching the back of Kyle's throat, Wes pulled back with a gasp. As sexy as it would be to watch this man take his load, he wanted something else.

Leaning down, he met Kyle's mouth in a hard kiss, tasting himself there. A groan caught in his throat and he pushed the other man down onto the flimsy mattress, climbing over top of him.

"I don't have any condoms," Kyle said breathlessly, and in a tone that made it clear he wasn't ready for that step yet.

Wes kissed him again, gently this time, his lips caressing Kyle's. The younger man relaxed beneath him and when they parted, that trusting expression returned.

God, what a dangerous look. He could get so very used to that.

"That's not what I'm after. Not right now," Wes panted, reaching down to grab ahold of Kyle's cock.

He positioned himself on top of the other man then rolled his hips, testing how close he was. Hot, needy flesh slid together, his cock over Kyle's, and he was rewarded with a muffled moan for his efforts.

Confident he had the right position, Wes made a loose fist around them both and thrust against Kyle, wordlessly encouraging him to do the same. They slid together, hips bucking and rolling, breaths coming in frantic bursts. At some point, Wes wasn't even aware of the noise he was making. He just needed this—needed release, but only after he saw Kyle get there.

It happened moments later, when Kyle tensed beneath him, the motion of his hips ceasing. His dick jerked in Wes' hand, and he shot between the two of them with a low, keening moan.

"That's it," Wes whispered, stealing another kiss. "Come for me."

Kyle was absolutely stunning, lips parted, head thrust back against the mattress, chest and arms glistening with sweat. It was enough to send Wes over the edge, and it only took one more thrust before he came just as hard, making a mess of things and ensuring they'd have to do some damage control before either of them left this room.

But as he lay there catching his breath, none of that mattered. Looking down at Kyle, he realized one terrifying fact: He hadn't gotten this man out of his system. Not in the slightest.

If anything, he wanted Kyle more, and that was a dangerous prospect.

14

KYLE

*I*f Kyle had ever need confirmation that he was absolutely, one hundred percent not straight, that little rendezvous in the on-call room would have been more than enough proof.

It wasn't something he wrestled with. It was just something he'd learned about himself a little later than other people might have learned it. So he was bi. Big deal. In Kyle's mind, that wasn't anything to angst over or even treat as much of a concern. He'd clearly always been bi, he'd just never found a man he was that attracted to that he was willing to make a move.

No, being bi wasn't the problem here. Fucking a colleague was the problem. Especially one who had such a high profile in the hospital and around town. It was impossible not to sometimes look at Wes like he was a perfectly-cooked steak and Kyle was a man starved. Their tryst in the on-call room had been one of the hottest experiences of his life, and he found himself daydreaming about it whenever he had downtime, to the point where Beth had noticed and asked what he was thinking about.

There was no way it wasn't all over the hospital by now. Just the fact that Wes didn't seem to treat him like all the other nurses was enough to get the rumor mill going. The looks the two exchanged every now and again were like pouring gasoline onto an already roaring fire.

And yet Kyle still didn't regret it. He had no idea where to go from there, and the next day was an exercise in awkward as he tried to sort out his interactions with Wes. But he still didn't regret it. They were both adults. They'd figure out what was probably just a bit of fun; a way to blow off steam amidst a stressful situation.

That was the hope Kyle relied on as he followed up with Wes' patients. There were only two who'd been admitted overnight, and both had stabilized well before they were given over to his care, so Kyle mostly tried to keep them comfortable and distracted until they could be discharged.

Around mid-morning—after catching Wes' eye for a half second and then fleeing back to his work like a coward—Kyle made his way to the nurses' station to update his charts.

"Kyle!"

He didn't recognize the voice at first. His brow furrowed and he looked around, only to see Brandon rushing down the hallway, his face awash with worry.

"Brandon? What's wrong?"

Katie. It had to be Katie. His pulse raced, his heart leaping into his throat as he tried to remember the cases he'd heard the others talking about today. There wasn't anything too severe—not that he remembered. But that didn't mean something wasn't very, very wrong.

"I'm freaking out, man," Brandon said, reaching the desk. An unnecessary admission, since he looked like he hadn't slept for a week. "I need your help. Please, Kyle."

So many scenarios raced through Kyle's mind, and the terror in Brandon's eyes wasn't helping matters any. His brother reached for him, grabbing the arm of his scrub shirt, and Kyle let himself be pulled down the hall by the frantic man.

You need to stay calm, he reminded himself. *Brandon and Katie need you to keep it together.*

But as soon as that curtain was thrown back to reveal a little girl with a tear-streaked face and a very swollen ankle, Kyle found his resolve crumbling. Realistically, he knew it wasn't anything serious. She was conscious and breathing and just from a quick visual assessment, it seemed like she'd maybe taken a tough spill or something. She was hurt, but she would be okay.

And yet for some reason, Kyle's mind latched on to all of the worse things that could have happened to his niece.

Trying to quash his initial reaction, he smiled at Katie and stepped into the exam space. "Looks like you did a number on your ankle."

"I tripped and fell," she said, not looking him in the eyes. "It's not that big of a deal."

As he stepped closer, Kyle realized the tear tracks were just stains. The fresh glimmer had faded a long time ago, and Katie's more relaxed attitude seemed genuine.

Brandon, however, was still a bundle of nerves. "She was in a lot of pain. And look at how big the swelling is! God, Kyle, what if it's broken?"

"Can I take a look? I promise I won't touch."

Katie nodded, her teeth snagging her lip. Despite her response, there was enough worry in her eyes to give Kyle a pretty good idea of what happened here. She'd gotten hurt and she was in pain and scared, but she was trying to be strong for her dad.

The least Kyle could do was to keep his shit together and not let himself worry about what was a very typical childhood injury.

Crouching down, he took a look at her ankle around the injury site, but stayed a good distance away from what was likely just a sprain. He was about to reassure them both of that when the curtain pulled back and a familiar voice greeted them.

"Mr. Harris," Wes said, and Kyle felt a shiver race up his spine despite himself. "And you must be Katie."

Kyle rose in time to see him tuck Katie's chart under one arm and offer a hand for Brandon to shake, then Katie. She looked up at him shyly, but took his hand and gave it a shake.

"I'm Dr. Monroe, and I'm going to do everything in my power to get you feeling better so you can get out of this place, okay?"

He spoke to her in a quiet, calm voice, an easy smile dominating his features. Even Kyle felt somewhat soothed by it.

"Was there someone in here before you came to get me, Bran?" he asked, getting to his feet so Wes had room to work.

"Yeah. Another nurse. I don't remember her name. She took Katie's blood pressure and temperature and everything," Brandon said, frazzled.

Without Kyle having to ask, Wes simply offered him the chart. His heart did a silly little flip in his chest, despite the fact that he knew the smile the man offered wasn't really for his benefit.

"So how did you hurt your ankle, Katie?" Wes asked, crouching the same way Kyle had.

She told the same brief story as before, though Brandon added it was during PE class.

"We were playing soccer," she admitted, tucking a strand of hair behind her ear. "I went to kick the ball and…"

She made a motion with her hand that told the rest of the story. Apparently she'd suffered a Charlie Brown style spill, but without the presence of a Lucy to blame it on. Kyle winced. No wonder she'd chosen to be a little stoic about the whole thing and downplay how much it hurt.

"Sure, that's one version of events. But I think it went down like this:"

Wes cleared his throat, and to Kyle it was a clear distraction from the gentle prodding he was doing at the site of the injury. It seemed to work, as Katie's attention was on him, not her ankle.

"I think you were going in for the slide tackle at just the right moment to keep the other team from scoring," Wes said as he carefully manipulated Katie's foot, "and right as you were about to connect," he paused for a moment and looked up at her, "who's your least favorite person in your class?"

Katie's cheeks flushed red, but she answered almost immediately. "Tyler."

Wes made a face. "Yeah. Nothing good ever came from a person named Tyler. I think you were just about to stop a scoring drive, and Tyler stuck out his stupid foot to trip you. That sound about right?"

A small, secret smile touched Kyle's lips even as he looked over the information Wes had taken down. Katie giggled, completely oblivious to the examination that was going on. Even Brandon seemed to relax a little.

"I wish I could say it happened that way," Katie lamented.

"I won't tell if you don't." Wes gave her a wink, then stood so he could address everyone in the room. "It's almost certainly a sprain. We can do an X-ray just to be safe, but I really don't see any evidence of a fracture."

"Would a sprain really swell that much?" Brandon asked, skeptically.

To Kyle's surprise, Wes didn't answer right away. Rather he looked to him, waiting patiently as Kyle finally understood he was being given a chance to answer his brother.

"They can. Especially in children. Since her range of movement isn't that limited, a sprain is a safe bet."

Brandon nodded, and Wes went on to explain the treatment plan. Rest, ice, compression, and elevation, mostly, but he was also going to give Katie a brace to help keep the ankle steady. With everything ordered, Wes made his way out of the room to see to his other patients, leaving Kyle to speak to his brother and niece alone.

"That's the doctor you were having problems with, isn't he?" Brandon asked almost immediately.

Kyle felt heat rise in his face as he wrote down Wes' orders. "Mostly resolved now."

"I see that."

His brother was obviously feeling better about the situation, because he was wearing the textbook definition of a shit-eating grin. Even Katie was looking at him like she knew something he didn't.

"What?" he asked the room, both brows lifting.

"Nothing." Brandon waved him off. "He just seems like a good man. Actually... will you thank him for me?"

A sudden flush colored Kyle's cheeks as he imagined just how he could thank Wes. Brandon definitely didn't need to know that, though, and so he just murmured his agreement and scrambled to fetch the brace. The sooner he could get Katie on her way, the sooner she'd be back to her old self. And honestly, he'd hoped to catch up with Wes at some point.

Whether it was luck or providence, he spotted Wes at the end of the hall and jogged to catch up with him. "Dr. Monroe," he called, amending it as he got closer. "Wes. Hold up."

Wes stopped, and those steely eyes fixed on Kyle with an intensity that took his breath away. Their last interaction might have been completely innocent, but just one look reminded him of the on-call room, and fire lit through his veins.

But he wasn't here for that, as much as his body disagreed. He'd wanted to find Wes for a very specific reason, and fortunately that reason didn't involve either of them being unclothed.

"I just wanted to thank you for what you did back there. Brandon was a wreck, and poor Katie was trying to keep it together for him. I tried to do what I could, but you just... came in and made everything better, in a matter of minutes."

"Part of the job," Wes said, though his expression softened considerably. "The biggest part, if you ask me."

He shrugged and made to leave, but Kyle reached out on a whim and grabbed his arm. Wes stopped, his gaze moving slowly from Kyle's hand to his eyes. It wasn't that heated, sexual gaze he'd given earlier, yet somehow it made him feel just as exposed.

"Thank you," Kyle said again. "It means a lot to me. I... haven't always been there for Brandon and Katie, so it's nice to see someone care about them. Even if it's just part of the job for you."

"It's not," he said after a moment. "It's not just part of the job. It *is* the job." His lips curved into a slow, almost sly, smile. "But on the other hand, Dr. Silverman was supposed to handle this case, and I'd be lying if I said I hadn't taken a special interest because of the last name."

Kyle let out a surprised, somewhat self-conscious laugh as he drew his hand back. What was he supposed to do with that, exactly? He'd never wanted special treatment, but he had to admit it felt... nice. The sentiment behind it, at least.

"If you want to thank me, though, I have an idea."

His throat became instantly parched, the smooth reach of those words stoking an ember that still smoldered within him. Wes could have asked him back to the on-call room at that moment, and he likely would have agreed.

Instead, he asked for something that was honestly pretty innocent.

"Meet me at the duck pond in Moore Wood after your shift." When Kyle gave him a confused look, he added, "We need someplace to talk about the hospital without everyone overhearing, right? And the sooner we can get a plan together, the sooner we can present it to Sloane."

Right. The hospital. The whole reason they'd started spending time together in the first place. Of course it wasn't anything else. Definitely not a date, as much as his stupid heart apparently leapt at the thought.

Why he was disappointed by that, Kyle didn't care to examine. He pushed it aside, summoning the most professional smile he could manage, and said, "I'll be there."

15

KYLE

*A*fter a quick check on Brandon and Katie—the latter of whom was enjoying ice cream as Brandon wrestled with parental guilt over his child being injured—Kyle made his way to Moore Wood, all of the research he'd gathered tucked neatly into a messenger bag.

He walked like a man with a purpose, striding from his car to the park's entrance, his gaze scanning the area for Wes as he followed the path to the duck pond. Inside, though, it was hard to think of the business that had brought him here. Nerves danced in his stomach and his heart did a ridiculous little flip the moment he spotted Wes, the tall man dressed in more casual clothing that reminded Kyle of the first night they'd met. Moonlight cast an almost silvery sheen against his jet-black hair and bathed his tanned skin with ambient light, making him look almost ethereal, and even more intimidating than normal.

The man turned, hands in his pockets, and smiled when he spotted Kyle. That expression did even stranger things to him, and he decided to counteract the awkwardness by blurting out his intent.

"I brought everything I've been researching for the past week," he patted his bag. "I thought we could go over it."

"Sure." Wes reached into his back pocket and pulled out his phone, swiping it to life to reveal a document. "I've got everything in here."

That was... a lot more practical, though Kyle had to wonder how Wes managed to get everything on that system. He was pretty sure the man hadn't updated the firmware since smart phones became a thing.

"There's a bench I like to sit at sometimes. One of my favorite places in town, actually."

Something strange was happening, because Kyle could swear Wes was actually nervous. It might have been a small thing to share something he enjoyed, but Kyle gathered that wasn't the case for him. Knowing that this spot meant so much to the older man, he knew he needed to tread carefully.

"Lead the way," he said with a smile, his heart thudding beneath his breast as he walked along with Wes, an awkward silence hanging between them.

It was broken, thankfully, when Wes asked, "Were you able to check on your niece?"

"She's fine," he answered with a laugh. "My brother's feeding her all the ice cream she can eat right now, but I think that's more for his benefit than hers."

"He seems like a good father. Attentive. Caring. I'd say Katie's in good hands."

Kyle nodded, his smile borne of bride. "Yeah, he's a good guy. He always has been. When we were kids, he used to volunteer to watch all of our younger cousins. It... drove me a little crazy, actually." He let out a chuckle, rubbing the back of his neck. "I wanted to hang out with my brother, not a bunch of five and six-year olds."

They walked along a path, coming closer and closer to a big, clear lake. Shafts of moonlight poured down from the clouds, glinting on the water's surface. Fireflies danced amidst the reeds, and Kyle found himself almost gaping at just how beautiful it was.

No, not just beautiful. There was something romantic about it all, a fact that flustered him to no end. Especially when Wes kept asking questions.

"You and your brother are close?"

A sharp pain lanced through his chest, dulling with the knowledge that it wasn't the first—or last—time he'd feel that stab of guilt. "We were. Not as much anymore. I... left home as soon as I had the chance, and I didn't really see him again until our dad died."

They walked in silence for a bit, passing several benches that seemed perfectly fine. Wes had a specific spot in mind, though, and Kyle just followed along, idly wondering if he was being wooed.

It was a ridiculous thought. Wesley Monroe wasn't the type of man who wooed someone—he knew that instinctively. And yet...

"It's just up here," Wes said, interrupting his thoughts. He gestured to a bench that sat just below a sycamore tree, on a small hill that overlooked the lake.

It was so beautiful, so pristine, that Kyle couldn't help but ask, "How'd you find this place?"

They took a seat, the bench not really that small, but small enough to excuse Wes' thigh pressing against his.

"I grew up nearby. My old house is less than a mile away," he said, indicating the direction past the lake. "I used to come out here when I needed to… think."

The word was strained, and Kyle's curiosity was piqued. "Busy house?"

"Something like that," Wes remarked. He pulled out his phone and, without missing a beat, said, "Let's see what you've got."

Kyle pulled his messenger bag onto his lap, withdrawing a file folder filled with printouts. Most were financial records, accounts of how much the hospital spent on various services, with significant columns highlighted while others were underlined and still others were circled.

The chaos made sense to Kyle, but looking at it now, he realized he was going to have to explain his madness.

"So I went through and looked at all the non-essential services that could be cut without anyone losing their jobs. That's what this is," he pointed to a highlighted portion. "The circles denote places we can scale back and still serve Hidden Creek's population, and the underlined sections are things that could actually use expansion."

Focused care for seniors, for example. Like many rural areas, Hidden Creek had a fairly high population of older residents, and the concentration in surrounding areas was even larger. In Kyle's experience, Hidden Creek Memorial really needed someone who was specially trained with seniors in mind.

But that was going to have to take a backseat for now. If they couldn't keep the doors open, everyone would suffer—especially the older population that had nowhere else to go.

Wes leaned over to share his phone screen, and Kyle tried to ignore the sheer warmth emanating from the man's body and how much it reminded him of their time in the on-call room. Wes radiated heat then, and it'd been an arousing and oddly comforting feeling to have the man's body over top of his.

But that was definitely not the point of this meeting, even if Wes had shown a very personal interest in his life. Kyle ran that rhetoric through his mind over and over as they compared notes, consolidating their ideas into something they could type up for Director Sloane.

For the most part, the ease of working with Wes settled those nerves that rattled through him. Wes was a big picture kind of person, Kyle was learning. A dreamer through and through. He wanted Hidden Creek Memorial to be the absolute best hospital, fully focused on patient care with no expenses spared. But Kyle was more rational, and he frequently had to scale back Wes' ideas to something that might have a chance of passing muster with a man who very clearly wanted to retire.

They worked well together. As well as they did in the exam room, and maybe even as well as they had in the on-call room.

The only "interruption"—if he could even call it that—was the fact that Wes interjected every now and again to ask him more about his family and himself. Did he grow up in Texas? Where did he end up going to school? Why had Brandon settled in Hidden Creek, of all places?

Some just seemed like idle curiosity. Maybe Wes was the type of person who didn't like silence. But there were a few questions thrown in there that made him wonder. Especially when he looked up to find two men walking along the shore of the lake, hand in hand, whispering to one another—something Wes was also watching with what Kyle could only describe as a somewhat wistful expression.

Finally, he just blurted out, "Is this a date? Did you trick me into going on a date with you?"

Was it really a trick if he would have said yes? Wait. Would he have said yes? It all seemed insane.

"I don't do dates," Wes said, confirming the absurdity of the whole situation. And then he smirked in that sexy, secretive way that let Kyle know he was in trouble. "But if I did, this would be a nice spot for one, you have to admit."

"Aside from the mountains of expense analysis," Kyle muttered, hefting the stack he'd rested in his lap.

"Aside from that."

Wes shifted beside him, almost seeming to squirm. Obviously Kyle was just projecting, because that wasn't remotely possible. Wes was confident. The alpha of the hospital. Alphas made others squirm beneath them. They didn't take part in the squirming themselves.

"It wasn't a date," Wes affirmed, glancing back at Kyle, "but it could be. We could get a bite to eat. Talk for a bit."

Kyle almost gaped at the man, feeling a blush rise in his cheeks. He was being wooed, whether it was intentional or not. And he found himself feeling... okay with that. Rebecca had never taken the time to show him she was interested. She'd made it clear that was his job in the relationship, and she just basked in his attention.

With Wes, things were oddly on more equal footing. Even when the man pinned him with one of those intense stares that made him feel like a hare caught inches away from a wolf's maw.

"Or we could grab some pizza or gyros and go back to my place."

"What about the report?" Kyle asked weakly, already knowing he didn't care. Not right now, at least.

"We can get it ready tomorrow. Not like Sloane's going to close the place overnight."

Wes leaned closer, his thigh pressed more fully against Kyle's, and for the first time Kyle saw just how nervous he was, too. There was a humanity in his eyes, an uncertainty that was endearing. And ultimately, that was what swayed him fully into the direction he'd already been leaning.

He wanted more of what had happened between them. More of Wes' hands and mouth on him. More of their bodies pressed together. More wanton exploration of this new facet of who he was. If the heat in Wes' steel grey eyes was any indication, he wanted all of that, too.

But that slight proof of vulnerability made it clear there was something more behind it. All the questions, all the interest, the genuine concern for his family earlier. It spoke to something deeper that Kyle was afraid to name... but not afraid to experience.

"I'd like that," Kyle said, almost breathless. The smile that suddenly bloomed on Wes' face was worth the tug of nervousness.

He stood from the bench and followed the man back to the parking lot, passing along the bank of that beautiful, moonlit lake, convinced now more than ever that Wes had planned this all along.

And not minding one bit.

16

WES

*D*inner was a simple affair. Wes called in an order and picked it up, urging Kyle to go ahead to his place and make himself comfortable. He'd given the man his key—a temporary gift, but one Kyle balked at—and sent him off in his own car. Partly because it was the practical thing to do, and partly because it gave him time to sort out his feelings.

Something was happening here. Something that felt a great deal bigger than anything Wes had prepared for or wanted. And somehow, he had the feeling that the way they chose to approach tonight would decide a great many things about the future.

Had he ever had that moment with Adrian? A point of no return? Their relationship had transitioned somewhat seamlessly, to the point that Wes barely even noticed he relied on Adrian so much. In fact, he wasn't sure he had noticed until it was too late.

It might not have been the same situation with Kyle, but he enjoyed the man's company. He liked working with him, and he was genuinely interested in learning more. For most people, that might not have signified, but for Wes—someone who'd made it very clear to everyone in Hidden Creek that he only did casual sex —it was huge.

He could walk away from it now. Kyle would be annoyed if he suddenly changed his mind, but he'd get over it. Alternately, he could forget about dinner and conversation entirely and just fuck the man senseless if Kyle was willing.

But both of those options felt wrong, and so Wes stuck to the original plan. He picked up their meals, then drove to his apartment where Kyle stood sheepishly by the sideboard, a bottle of wine in his hands with a corkscrew stuck inside.

Wes snorted at the sight. "Having trouble there?"

"Okay, in my defense, this corkscrew is from like... 1912 or something."

"I'll trade you," Wes' lips curved into a smirk as he held up the takeout bag. "There are plates in the cabinet closest to the stove, and silverware in the second drawer."

Kyle made a face at that. "You're one of those people who dumps takeout onto an actual plate, huh?"

He took the bag and Wes went to pry the corkscrew out of the cork. "Not normally. Normally I eat them hunched over the steering wheel with a plastic spork. But since this isn't a date..."

He heard Kyle laugh from the kitchen, and shortly after, the cork finally popped free. The wine could've used time to breathe, but Wes' nerves were so overwrought that he decided to pour it immediately, adding a generous amount to two glasses.

After a bit of fussing—and a lot of scraping of silverware on plates —Kyle came out of the kitchen with two plates and associated silverware.

"Compromise? It feels weird to eat takeout at a dinner table. And

—this may be hard to believe—but nobody's ever going to mistake my plating techniques for a master chef's."

He was right about that. The best Wes could say about the plating was that the entree was mostly kept separate from the sides. Not that he minded. Residency had taught Wes to eat what he could when he could, and any pickiness he had over eating was resolved quickly in his first year.

"You're not going to hear any complaints from me," he said, gesturing to the couch.

They settled in, wine glasses on end tables, plates on laps. It was an odd mix of formal and casual, but somehow it worked. Wes' nerves eased somewhat, and after half a glass of wine, he was feeling more like himself and less like a teenager who'd just realized he had a crush on a boy at school.

Kyle seemed to relax, as well. While they'd talked about random, safe things throughout the meal, it was obvious there was something on Kyle's mind. After a bit more wine, he finally gave it voice.

"I... have a question you're not going to like very much."

"Know me that well, do you?" Wes smirked, but his heart started beating at an irregular pace.

"Why do you have such a problem with nurses? I've seen who you are with the patients, and it just doesn't fit."

A fair enough question, but it conjured a mixed bag of memories that made Wes' food suddenly much harder to stomach. He lifted his wine glass to his lips and drained it, pouring himself more soon after.

He could give Kyle a vague answer and leave it at that. He was a controlling person—he always had been. He'd made so many hard decisions for his mother when he was young—all of them when she was fall-down drunk—that he'd never been comfortable letting go. But there was more to it than that, and as he looked at Kyle, he thought perhaps the man deserved to know the full story.

"When I was doing my residency, I fell for a patient," he began, his finger scraping along the edge of the glass. "Not one of mine, and not while he was being treated. It happened afterward." A soft smile touched his lips as he remembered running into the confident man who'd apparently decided from day one that he and Wes were meant to be together. "His name was Adrian. He was... an amazing man with a very unfortunate medical condition."

He could feel the shift in the room. No doubt Kyle had picked up on the pointed use of "was," but Wes just didn't have it in him to hide the sorrow or the bitterness.

"What was wrong with him?" the man asked softly.

Wes let out a humorless laugh. "His heart was too big. Literally. Genetically. It was too much of an effort for his body to maintain."

Adrian joked about it all the time. It was one of his favorite anecdotes to throw out into a room and see how people reacted. Even when he was hospitalized, he kept that same disposition. It was something Wes deeply admired about the man, and one of the reasons he'd loved him so much. He was a light in the darkness... until that light was finally snuffed out.

"He must've been on medications though," Kyle said weakly, his brow set in a deep crease.

"He was, but even the maintenance wasn't a perfect solution. He ended up in the hospital a few times a year, and he used to tease me about how hands-on I'd get," Wes said with a bitter smile, taking another long drink of wine. "But I needed to be doing something to help. It was agony to just sit in that chair beside his bed and watch him suffer."

Kyle reached across the couch and laid a hand atop Wes', giving it a gentle squeeze. "No one likes feeling helpless."

"No, but apparently it's necessary sometimes." A harsh note tinged his words as the memories surfaced. They'd treated him like he was any other worried love one; like he didn't have a clue what Adrian needed. "My last year as a resident, Adrian spent almost two months in the hospital. We were considering adding him to the transplant list, but one night while I was getting a bit of rest at home, he started having complications. He was in cardiac arrest by the time I got back to the hospital, and I demanded to go in with the other doctors. They wouldn't let me." Wes squared his jaw, looking away from Kyle. "One of the nurses escorted me out of the room and made me sit there while he died."

He'd been in the waiting room, too far away to watch what happened within. Afterward, he'd demanded exhaustive details. Who called the code? Who responded first? What meds did they try and in what quantities? What life-saving measures did they attempt, and how long did they keep going?

Because if Wes was in the room, he would have kept going until he collapsed.

"I know you might not understand. It probably sounds petty to you," Wes admitted quietly. It wasn't a worry he'd ever said aloud before, but there it was, existing in the space between them.

"It doesn't sound petty. Losing a loved one so suddenly... Wes, I can't imagine what that's like. But I do know that the people with you—the people who break the news—stay in your mind whether it's a conscious memory or not. You felt helpless. Out of control.

There was nothing you could do for Adrian, and the people you trusted were actively keeping you away from him." Kyle gave his hand another squeeze. "I get that."

His gaze settled on their hands, and Wes felt that familiar pang of loss; of loneliness. He hadn't expected Kyle to argue with him about his own feelings, but he had expected some kind of well-meaning lecture. The fact that he wasn't receiving that right now meant more than he could say.

He finally looked at the man who sat beside him, Kyle's eyes softened with the same boundless empathy he'd seen him bestow upon their patients. It was caring. Compassion. A regard for Wes' wellbeing that he'd rarely felt. Mostly because he rarely let anyone else care for him in that way.

A part of him wanted to pull away; shore up and ask Kyle to leave before he saw anything more. Another part of him wanted to lean in to the man's embrace and accept what he was offering.

When Kyle leaned in and pressed his lips to Wes', he settled for something in between those two extremes. It was a concession of sorts. An admission that he needed the comfort, without letting himself surrender too much to it.

This he understood. The caress of lips, the searching of tongues, the heat of bodies intertwining. He didn't want to pretend like nothing had changed since that first night, he just wanted to explore it in a language that was easier to understand. In a language where he didn't feel weak and vulnerable and helpless.

And though Kyle's initial kiss was soft and comforting, he warmed to it as Wes did, a silent understanding passing between them.

They both needed this. For different reasons, he was sure, but in this instance, Wes was willing to be selfish and look after his own needs right now. And what he needed—more than anything else at this moment—was someone to treat him with the same warmth and compassion he knew Kyle was capable of giving.

17

KYLE

*I*t wasn't hard to understand what Wes needed: A distraction, for starters. And end to a conversation he obviously hadn't planned on having. Frankly, Kyle was just fine with that. As intrigued as he was about Wes' past and what had made him the way he was, there was only so much heaviness he was prepared to handle. Especially when those steely eyes turned gray and sad, the same color as an overcast day when all you wanted was to see the sun again.

Kyle felt that pain too keenly to do anything other than respond, and when his arms came around Wes, they were offered in comfort much more than desire. The kiss was given with an understanding that this would help Wes heal in some way, and helping others heal was what Kyle had dedicated his life to doing.

There was more to it than that, though. If he looked back on this night and thought of it as something he simply did for Wes, he would be able to make peace with that. But this wasn't just for Wes. Kyle needed this, too. He craved the touch of someone who actually wanted him. Someone who wasn't stringing him along, too much of a coward to end things before their wedding day. He needed the intensity in Wes' gaze because it reminded him that he was worth that kind of attention and devotion.

He wasn't fooling himself. This wasn't the be-all, end-all. It wasn't going to be a joining together of two souls who would never experience hardship or strife. But it was the beginning of something, of that he was certain.

So when Wes pressed closer to him, Kyle held him tighter, easing down on the couch so that his neck rested against the arm of it, his body nestled against the cushions. His fingers curled against Wes' shirt, pulling him down so he could feel the hard planes of the other man's body against his own—and the harder ridge of his erection as it bulged through his slacks.

The friction as Wes moved above him was enough to send a molten shot of lust through him, though the emotions that still swelled beneath his breastbone helped keep him grounded. A little less so, when Wes started dragging his lips over Kyle's jaw, tracing a path to his ear and sucking the lobe into his mouth.

Kyle moaned, arching up against the man, his hands moving to the thick leather belt at his waist. He struggled with the buckle, undoing it and pulling the belt free from the loops that were easiest to reach. The slacks sagged slightly on Wes' body, and Kyle took advantage of that to pull the light blue dress shirt free, stubbornly ignoring the buttons.

Wes continued to torture him throughout, offering no help whatsoever as he sought out sensitive spots along Kyle's neck. He found one where shoulder met neck, and exploited it to its fullest after Kyle's gasp, licking and sucking and even applying the light scrape of teeth.

"I'm trying to concentrate here," Kyle said in weak protest.

He felt the gust of warm breath on his neck as Wes laughed. "Just rip the thing off. I'll get the buttons sewn back on later."

Before Kyle could say anything, Wes captured his mouth in a hungry kiss that only served to stoke those fires even more. Kyle moaned into the man's mouth, savoring the taste of wine and Wes, every other need forgotten in that moment.

At least until he remembered he'd been given free rein to ruin Wes' clothes. Grabbing from the bottom of the shirt, he pulled the sides in two different directions, the give of it all too satisfying as buttons pinged off every which way.

Wes complied with another deep rumble of a laugh, sitting up with his knees resting on either side of Kyle's hips. He shrugged out of the destroyed garment and whipped his belt off to the side where it landed with a heavy thud and clink. Large hands with long, dexterous fingers set upon Kyle's chest, making their intent clear.

"I'll lend you a shirt," was the only warning Wes gave before doing the exact same thing—ripping Kyle's shirt open with such a ridiculously sexy flourish that he swore he felt his dick twitch in response.

Kyle leaned up just enough to get the shirt off his shoulders and arms, but Wes put a hand on his chest and pushed him back down while he was still tangled in the garment. He followed it up with a forceful kiss, and Kyle surrendered, his hands tangling in the man's thick, dark hair.

He was far from passive, though, lifting his ass off the couch and rolling his hips against Wes'. The other man groaned, momentarily thrown off his path of dominance, a shuddered breath escaping him. Kyle bit back a smirk and was "rewarded" for his defiance when Wes reached between them to undo his belt, too, casting it aside.

He lifted up on his knees again, his eyes intense and filled with lust; desire that was completely directed at Kyle. No one else. The feeling of it rushed through him, getting into his blood and pulsing through his veins, warming him from the inside out until he felt like he was on fire.

Sitting astride him, Wes undid the button of his pants and tugged down the fly. Kyle's cock pulsed in anticipation, a shiver racing through his body as Wes' hand came closer, finally pulling him free.

He stroked slowly, from root to tip, making eye contact with Kyle the whole time. "Tell me what you like."

"That's a good start," Kyle said weakly.

Honestly, he wasn't sure what he liked. He'd had his dick handled before, even sucked, but never the thorough, attentive way Wes did it. It always seemed like a chore to his female partners, so he'd eventually just stopped asking.

But Wes relished every moment of it, lavishing him with attention from the slow tugs and squeezes to the way his thumb sought out sensitive flesh and exploited it, rubbing over the head of his cock.

"There," Kyle gasped, when Wes pressed just below the crown, stimulating that sensitive bit of flesh that connected the head to the rest of his cock.

Wes didn't immediately follow through, though. Instead he pushed himself up from the couch and moved the coffee table out of the way, silverware clattering to the floor. Kyle reached for his aching dick, watching as Wes shucked off his pants, a prominent bulge in his briefs.

The man was lightning-fast when he noticed, though, grabbing Kyle's wrist and pinning it behind his head. "I get you off. Understood?"

He just nodded, eyes half-lidded as Wes pulled off Kyle's pants and boxers, leaving him bare on the man's couch. He dropped down to the carpeted floor then, his mouth immediately attending to Kyle's cock, tongue tracing along the crown as his hand moved down to cup Kyle's balls.

The siege continued with Wes drawing him inches into his mouth, his lips pressed tight below the head, his fingers stroking the seam of Kyle's sac. He moaned and squirmed, unable to keep his hips from bucking or his hands from fisting in Wes' hair. The moment he did, though, Wes used his upper body strength to pin him down and took him to the root, leaving Kyle gasping for breath.

Just when he thought he wasn't going to be able to handle any more, Wes one-upped himself again. The man's hands gripped his legs, turning him on the couch and then lifting his unclothed limbs up. He braced them there, one arm beneath Kyle's thighs as he used his free hand to massage his cheek. He honestly had no idea what Wes intended until he felt hot breath somewhere he'd definitely never felt it before.

He must have tensed, because Wes looked at him in question, then murmured a simple, "Trust me," before continuing on.

He felt the tip of Wes' wet, searching tongue as it probed around the sensitive skin, setting his nerves aflame with anticipation. Wes circled his hole several times, to the point where Kyle wasn't expecting it any longer when that deft and powerful tongue finally pressed inside of him.

He gasped, torn between pulling away and pushing back against Wes. Kyle was pretty sure he did both, but Wes' arms just wrapped around his thighs to hold him in place as he pressed in again, deeper this time. Pleasure arced through Kyle in violent bursts, his hands gripping hard in Wes' hair as he let out a string of unintelligible curses—or what he thought were supposed to be curses, at least.

He was so close and his balls ached with the need for release, but he obeyed Wes' command, keeping himself from jacking off in time to the man's talented tongue. God, if it felt this good to have Wes' tongue inside him, how would it feel to have his cock hitting that spot again and again?

The thought made a full-body shudder course through him, his anticipation coiling even tighter as his muscles tensed. Wes must have sensed this, because he snuck one hand over Kyle's thigh and gripped his cock with the confidence of a man who knew he was going to get what he wanted.

"Oh, God," Kyle moaned, so close to the edge he almost couldn't stand it.

Wes redoubled his efforts, his face buried between Kyle's cheeks as he undertook a single-minded mission to make him come. To say that mission was a success would have been a severe understatement, as Kyle was soon wracked by one of the most violent orgasms of his life, his hips bucking, hot cum spurting from his cock and landing to cool on Wes' arms and Kyle's own body.

His mouth was held open in a silent expression of bliss for several moments, and when his muscles finally relaxed, he let out a long, drawn-out moan that nearly turned to a whimper as he watched Wes lick the cum off his arm.

"Fuck," he gasped, his head falling back.

Wes didn't give him much respite. Though he gently lowered Kyle's legs—a good thing, since his muscles felt like jelly—he kissed and licked a trail up Kyle's chest, cleaning off every last drop before his mouth met Kyle's. He groaned into the kiss, drawing back just enough to murmur against Kyle's lips.

"We can end this here if you're not ready for more," he stole another kiss and Kyle responded eagerly, despite his fatigue.

"No," Kyle breathed. "I want this. I want you."

It was the answer Wes must have wanted to hear, because the man kissed him with a hunger that almost made Kyle dizzy. And somehow—despite having just had the most intense orgasm of his life—he could already feel the blood pumping south.

"Not here," Wes said, and then he was pushing himself to his feet, his still-clothed cock straining against his briefs.

He pulled Kyle up with him, chest to chest, hips to hips, and mouths and tongues met in a needy dance. Wes' hands moved down his back to his ass, squeezing firmly, drawing Kyle close to him.

Somehow—over the course of what seemed like an hour, but was probably ten minutes or so—they managed to stumble their way toward Wes' bedroom, taking advantage of walls and tables that were in their path.

Wes pushed Kyle down on the soft bed, letting him scooch up as he finally tugged off his briefs. Wes' thick, beautiful cock sprang free, impressively—and probably painfully—hard, and Kyle felt his mouth water. One taste and he'd apparently become an addict.

Moving to the edge of the bed, he took charge before Wes could, gripping the other man's dick at the base and taking the head into his mouth. Wes groaned, his hands moving to Kyle's hair. Fingers clenched automatically, holding tight, directing Kyle's actions before he stopped himself and relaxed. But a thrill shot through Kyle in those few moments, his body and mind reacting to that sudden loss of control as Wes dictated his actions. It was oddly intoxicating, and he lifted his gaze to the man and tried to make him understand.

When that didn't seem to work, Kyle pulled back with a gasp, Wes' cock glistening with his saliva, and said, "I'll tell you if I need you to ease up."

Wes searched his eyes for a moment, then nodded, his fingers curling into Kyle's wavy hair once more. This time, he didn't wait for Kyle to take him into his mouth. He thrust forward, pushing the head past Kyle's lips, then pumped his hips in shallow motions, feeding him a few inches before drawing back.

It wasn't something Kyle thought he'd ever enjoy. He wasn't a control freak, but he liked being on top of things. Here, though, it was like sharing a deeper intimacy with Wes. He trusted that the man wasn't going to do anything he didn't want; that he'd stop the moment Kyle told him to. Because of that, the forced loss of control felt almost liberating. He was almost an outside observer to Wes' overwhelming desire for him, and not concentrating on his technique gave him a chance to appreciate the velvety texture of the man's cock as it slid past his lips, the weight and heat of it in his mouth, the subtle taste of salt and musk, and the low, needy sounds Wes made as he fucked Kyle's mouth.

Just because Wes held the control right now didn't mean he had to be completely passive, though. As he gained confidence, Kyle gripped Wes' ass and held him in place, taking him deeper than Wes had allowed so far. The man moaned, his grip tightening in Kyle's hair, but he didn't pull away. And when Kyle finally let up, Wes pumped deeper, faster, challenging Kyle to keep pace.

It ended sooner than he would have liked, as Wes suddenly pulled out with a curse. "Fuck. I'm not going to last."

He wouldn't have minded that, honestly, but his mind slowly caught up with Wes' meaning. He wanted more before he came, and so did Kyle. His dick was firming again, and the motion of Wes' thrusts made him ache for something he couldn't explain. He watched as Wes moved around the bed, the put-together man almost fumbling with the drawer of his bedside table. Kyle caught the flash of metallic wrappers and a white bottle, and his muscles tensed in anticipation.

"On your back," Wes said, the words spoken gently, but still a command as he rolled the condom over his dick.

Kyle complied, finding himself grateful for the direction. His whole body practically vibrated with tension, and his mind wasn't exactly helping him. Moments ago, he'd been lost in lust and willing to let Wes shove his cock all the way down his throat if he wanted. Now, he was worried about how his underused—or never-used, in this case—muscles would take it. Pain was something he expected, sort of, but he wasn't exactly prepared for it, or how he'd react if it was too much. All those worries and more tangled in his mind, fighting with his desire for the very thing he'd said he wanted.

It was impossible for Wes not to take notice.

"Nervous?" he asked, no sign of a smirk or any other condescension on his face.

"Not at all. Definitely not nervous about you putting your very big dick in my ass. Did it grow another few inches while I wasn't looking?" he asked with a nervous laugh. "It looks bigger now."

Wes let out a soft snort, and Kyle watched as the man's hand fisted around his cock, slowly stroking to keep himself hard. "First off, thanks for noticing. Second... we don't have to do this if you aren't ready for it."

A pang of sharp, sudden emotion clenched just behind Kyle's chest. Even that first night, Wes had backed off when Kyle needed him to—something he really hadn't expected with how he came across. It was nice to see that even in the heat of the moment, he was putting his partner's comfort and consent first.

Resting his elbows on the bed, Kyle leaned up and reached for Wes, his hand behind the man's neck. He drew him into a soft, grateful kiss and smiled as it broke.

"No. I want this. Just... go slow?"

Wes brushed his lips across Kyle's once more and climbed onto the bed, the sudden shift of weight filling Kyle with a mix of anxiety and excitement. He tried to focus on the latter, especially when Wes got onto his knees, his hands moving over Kyle's thighs as he caressed them, gently nudging them apart.

He heard the squirt of the lube bottle before he felt the slightly cold substance as Wes spread it liberally between his cheeks. His fingers remained, teasing around his hole until one slid deftly inside with more ease than Kyle expected. He moaned softly as Wes slowly moved his finger in and out, the lubrication ceasing to be cold after a few moments.

Removing his finger, Wes replaced it with the head of his cock resting right at his entrance, the tip of the condom just barely brushing his skin. He shivered, looking up at Wes in question. The man gave him a smile in return and returned his hands to Kyle's thighs.

"Just tell me if you need me to stop," he said before pushing the head of his cock past the tight ring of Kyle's hole.

There was a bit of pressure, but nothing too bad. He let out the breath he'd been holding and nodded to Wes, giving him permission to continue. The man's cock pushed in deeper, leading to a slow sense of fullness that Kyle had never experienced before. It wasn't unpleasant by any means, and as he adjusted to it, he found he actually liked it. The heat of Wes' cock, the feel of it throbbing inside of him, the resistance and friction as he drove deeper.

He felt a little discomfort the more he took, and Wes wasn't able to bottom out before Kyle had to stop him. But then he started to move in earnest, drawing back and pushing forward with shallow strokes, angling himself in the perfect way to hit Kyle's prostate every time, and any discomfort was gone. Bliss took over, sharp and sudden and shooting through his body all the way to the tips of his fingers.

Wes pumped his hips in a restrained manner, knowing exactly what he was doing, and Kyle writhed as his body became a vessel for pleasure. The effect was only aided by Wes reaching past his legs to grip his cock, stroking him in time with his thrusts.

A deep moan poured from him, the sound resonating in a way Kyle had never heard before. It almost didn't sound like him, but Wes certainly responded to it.

"That's it, baby," he said in a low, growly voice, his pace picking up in response.

Wes pushed deeper, his cock filling and stretching Kyle and driving him a little crazy. He pushed back against the man, suddenly more wanton than he'd ever been in his life, and desperate for more. Wes squeezed his cock—punishment or acknowledgment, Kyle wasn't sure which—and drove harder, his heavy balls slapping against Kyle's ass, their thighs meeting again and again, the mattress rocking, headboard pounding the wall under the abuse.

Wes' hand flew over his cock, stroking insistently, demanding him to let go. After a while, he couldn't fight it. He felt that familiar tightness in his balls and a tension in his muscles that begged to be released.

"Oh God, I'm—"

His whole body shuddered and spasmed, his dick jerking as he came hard. That sensation was more than enough to wrack his body with pleasure, but Wes wasn't letting up. He pounded into Kyle with no restraint, fucking him hard enough that he was sure he'd have bruises on the backs of his thighs tomorrow.

Kyle arched against him, his ass clenching around Wes' cock again and again. That must have been enough to do the other man in, because he buried himself deep within Kyle's body and let out a half-shout, half-roar of pleasure, his dick pulsing, drawing out every last ounce of pleasure.

As Kyle finally came back to his senses, he looked up at Wes to find the man's sexy, well-defined body glistening with sweat. His hair was matted to his forehead and he was panting, his hips still jerking involuntarily, his hands a little shaky on Kyle's thighs.

It was one of the sexiest things Kyle had ever seen, and when the man pulled out of him and discarded the condom, Kyle was quick to draw him back in for a heated kiss. Wes laughed against him, threading his fingers through Kyle's sweat-dampened hair. When the kiss broke, he rested his forehead against Kyle's, prompting another sharp squeeze of his heart.

"So I'm guessing you didn't hate that," he said with a chuckle.

Kyle smacked him lightly on the arm. "Ass."

He waggled his brows and slid his arms around Kyle, drawing him close. While Kyle had always enjoyed the intimacy of cuddling after sex, he definitely hadn't expected Wes to enjoy it. Just another way he'd misjudged the man, he supposed, and as he settled into Wes' embrace, he found himself looking forward to all the new discoveries the future would bring.

18

WES

*W*aking the next morning with his arms still wrapped around Kyle was almost surreal. It'd been so long since anyone had spent the night; since he'd even wanted that from another man. The people he'd brought back to his apartment were meant to fulfill a need, and once that need was met, they left. Obviously in a small town it was impossible not to see some of them again, but Wes had thus far done an admirable job of separating his private persona from the one he presented to the public.

The lines were blurred with Kyle, though. They had been from the start, when he'd seen a glimpse of the other man's vulnerability. It was only more complicated now, because while last night had been one of the better sexual experiences of his life, it'd also been borne of an emotional need he couldn't deny.

It might have been easy for the Wes of the past to just shower and leave with the expectation that Kyle would lock up, but the thought of doing so made something twist in his chest. It felt deeply wrong, so much so that he was slammed with guilt for even thinking it.

Instead, he lay in bed, watching the slow rise and fall of Kyle's chest until his phone went off at five thirty, sounding the morning alarm. Kyle groaned, looking at him bleary-eyed with a shy, sleepy smile that Wes was forced to respond to, his lips brushing over the other man's.

A shared shower might have been his next preference, but they didn't have time. A presentation needed to be readied for Sloane, and he took turns fixing breakfast with Kyle, the younger man taking the first shower shift, Wes taking the second. By the time they were both clean, the bacon, eggs, and toast were done and they sat at his kitchen table, talking about their future plans for the hospital as though it were completely normal.

Gathering their best pieces of data, they agreed to speak with Sloane in the evening, before the director left for the day. The chance of seeing each other for more than a few moments at a time was slim to none, so everything was solidified beforehand, and they left in their respective cars to face what was likely to be a hectic Sunday.

Neither of them had prepared for the reality of it.

Outside of working alongside him, getting vitals and administering care, Wes barely saw Kyle. There wasn't time for a lunch break. There was barely enough time to take a piss. From the moment he'd walked through the door until roughly five in the evening—an hour before Sloane was supposed to leave for the day —Wes was slammed. Case after case, patient after patient, from those who'd toughed out a cold over the weekend, all the way to a stroke.

When he'd finally caught up with the new patients, there were rounds to attend to, but Wes searched for Kyle first. They had a limited amount of time to speak to Sloane—especially since the man had a habit of ducking out early. It would be best to go now, when the proverbial sky wasn't falling.

Kyle, however, was nowhere to be found. But Wes did spot Sloane, briefcase in hand as he headed down the stairs.

"Tom!" he called, rushing toward the stairwell, past an orderly who was pulling a cart of supplies out of a closet.

"Oh, Wes. I was hoping I'd catch you," he said, the lack of eye contact suggesting anything but, "I wanted to give you a heads up that the Horn is going to announce the closure tomorrow, so things might get a little... crazy around here."

Wes just stared at the man, taken aback by so many parts of that statement that he had no clue where to start. The most egregious oversight seemed like the logical place, though. "You told the press before telling your employees?"

"It's better if everyone hears it from one place," Tom said, still avoiding eye contact. "It's not like we can shut down the hospital and call everyone into the cafeteria for a meeting. People would have to find out through the grapevine, anyway."

Wes shook his head, too astounded to say anything. At least until Sloane made his way further down the stairs, toward the exit.

"Wait," he called, before realizing he hadn't brought the packet with him. Kyle had it, tucked safely in his locker. But if he let Sloane leave now, the information would never make it to the paper. "I need to talk to you about the closure. I think there's a way we can keep the doors open without running you further into debt."

Tom looked down at his watch, shooting a wistful glance to the door. "I told June I'd be out of here before six, Wes. It's our anniversary today, did you know that?"

Of course it was his anniversary on the day when all of Hidden Creek had devolved into a complete meltdown—one that would continue once that story ran.

"Happy anniversary," Wes managed, moving to block Tom's retreat. "This won't take more than fifteen minutes, I swear."

Sloane glanced at his watch one more time, sighed, then said, "All right, Wesley." He gestured up the stairs. "You know the way."

Wes went first, half convinced Sloane was going to bolt if he didn't keep an eye on the man. It was too much of a risk to get Kyle. He'd have to do this alone. Then again, he'd known Tom Sloane most of his life—the good, the bad, and the ugly. If anyone was equipped to win the man over, it was Wes.

Once they were in his office, Tom closed the door and moved to make himself comfortable behind his desk, his slight beer belly catching on the edge of it before he adjusted his chair.

"Let's hear it, then," Tom said, moving his mouse around to wake up his ancient computer.

"I've been looking through the financial records with Kyle Harris—"

"—the nurse?" Tom asked, his gaze fixed on the screen. "Never thought I'd see the day."

"—and we've found some areas where the hospital is over-spending. There are programs and facilities that can be cancelled and closed that will cut back almost twenty percent of what it takes to run this hospital annually."

"And how many people have to lose their jobs for that?" he asked.

Again Wes was rendered speechless for a moment. If the hospital closed, everyone would lose their jobs. Some might be rehired when the county turned the building into a regional branch or walk-in clinic, but it would be a fraction of the people working there.

Rather than focus on that, though, he continued. "Ideally no one. We can shift a few positions around, automate a couple processes, stop funneling utilities to parts of the hospital that aren't used." Still the man wasn't looking at him, so Wes put his hands-on Sloane's desk and leaned forward, making himself unavoidable. "We've run the numbers, Tom. This'll work. The hospital can stop treading water. And if we do something in the community—a fundraiser or auction or something—the costs can be set right a lot sooner. You can even hire someone to manage things part-time, so you can spend more time with June."

Finally Sloane looked up at him, and Wes saw the first spark of hope he'd seen in the man for nearly a week. "This is an honest-to-God plan, son? Not some pipe dream?"

"Have a financial analyst run it if you need to, but it's solid. Hidden Creek Memorial doesn't have to close, as long as you don't want it to."

And if he did? Wes hadn't thought of a plan for that, and he hadn't wanted to raise the possibility with Kyle. Tom was nearing the age of retirement. His wife wanted him home. Closing the hospital was a clean, easy way to ensure his own future—at the cost of the town.

Maybe his faith was unfounded. Wes had never been one to trust beyond a shadow of a doubt, but years ago, Tom Sloane gave him a chance. He saw something in Wes no one else did, and he'd done everything in his power to nurture that and keep Wes in Hidden Creek so the community could benefit from his talent and dedication.

That was the man he needed to come through for the hospital, and that was the man he desperately hoped to see.

"Get me the papers," he said. "If it's like you say, then we'll do it."

Wes let out the breath he'd been holding before another concern struck him. "And the press release?"

"If this'll honestly be enough to keep the doors open, I'll call Matt tonight and make sure he puts it in the article." There was a spark in his eyes that hadn't been there before; a smile Wes recognized from the man's younger days. "Maybe he can help us with the community bit, too, that way people'll feel like they can do something about it when they get the news."

Wes' heart felt lighter than it had in a very long time, and the one person he wanted to share it with... was Kyle. A smile crept across his face, and he started toward the door. "I've still got ten minutes out of those fifteen you promised me. Let me get Kyle and the papers."

"Make it twenty minutes," Tom said, waving him off.

"What about your anniversary?"

"If this gets me home more often, June'll understand." Sloane made a shooing gesture, and Wes hurried out of the office, making his way toward the stairs.

They'd done it. It might not have been set in stone, but it still felt like a massive victory, and he couldn't wait to tell Kyle.

KYLE

*K*yle stopped his pacing long enough to look down at his phone. No new messages from Wes, which meant he was still doing rounds or dealing with an emergent case. He paced again, stopping just long enough to take a chug from his third Red Bull of the day as he tried to decide if he should go looking for the man. Six o'clock was nearing, and they were going to lose the chance to talk to Sloane soon.

The door to the break room swung open and a thrill shot through Kyle, adrenaline spiking his blood stream. It dropped instantly when he realized it was just Beth, though.

"Oh hey, sugar. Crazy out there today, huh? It's like the world's punishing me for taking a little vacation." She let out a dramatic sigh before her features turned serious, "I still can't believe what happened to Bottom's Up. And I can't believe Viv didn't call me and tell me when it happened!"

"Yeah, I can't imagine," Kyle said, mustering up the appropriate amount of sympathy.

It wasn't that he didn't care—he absolutely did. He might not have lived in Hidden Creek long, but Bottom's Up was a fixture in the town. More than a local watering hole, it was a public, safe space for people from every walk of life to come together and unwind after a long day.

But the bar could be rebuilt. If the hospital closed, there wasn't any re-opening it. Not without an absurd amount of money, and not with the same staff.

He started pacing again, not even realizing he was doing it until Beth said something.

"Are you... okay?" She came closer and lowered her voice. "I know it's none of my business," the exact phrase someone said right before making it their business, "but is something going on between you and Dr. Monroe?"

Kyle couldn't help but gape at her, unsure how to answer or if he even should. He knew Beth was a gossip, but just barging in on his personal life under the guise of concern?

"It doesn't matter to me one way or the other, but some of us have noticed he doesn't give you the same kinda shit he gives us. Maybe it's just 'cause you're new." She waved it off with a laugh. "It's probably that. You know what, forget I said anything."

"Yeah. Okay," Kyle said, planning to do just that.

Beth opened her locker, and for a second he thought he was in the clear. But of course, her head poked back out and she wore a pinched expression that conflicted with her smile.

"It's just, if you are—and it doesn't bother me one bit, like I said—but if you are, honey, you gotta know Wesley Monroe is kind of a player." She leaned in again, her tone turning conspiratorial. "My friend Janine said he seduced one of her nephews, and then slept with the other one the next night."

Kyle's mild annoyance started to turn to anger. He couldn't help it. He liked Beth, but this was none of her business. And what did it matter if Wes had apparently fucked some random guy and that guy's brother?

It wasn't like Kyle was looking for a commitment. They'd spent the night together. And it'd been… a more intimate experience than he'd ever had with anyone else in his life. But so what? He didn't have any claims on Wes.

Not unless he wanted to, and Kyle wasn't even sure where to begin with that. He'd just gotten out of a long-term relationship. Going home with Wes that first night had been a direct result of his heartache and a desire for something different. Was he really ready to demand more than sex? Was he in any position to do so?

And why the hell was he even thinking about this when he and Wes had approximately ten minutes to talk to Sloane?

"I appreciate the concern," Kyle lied, "but—"

Before he could finish, the door swung open again. This time it was Wes, his white coat abandoned somewhere, the dress shirt he'd picked out in the morning hugging his chest and shoulders in just the right way, and that smile… good lord. He'd never seen Wes smile like that, and it was absolutely captivating. Magnetic, even. So much so that he completely forgot about Beth.

Until she reminded them both she was still there.

"Oops, that's my cue. See you tomorrow, Kyle. Doctor."

There was a snideness to her tone Kyle didn't care for, but Wes completely ignored it, crossing the room to reach him. Once Beth was gone, his hands settled at either side of Kyle's face and he kissed him. Out of nowhere. And not just a peck, either. A full-on kiss that left Kyle as breathless as he was startled.

"We did it," Wes said, his voice almost giddy. "Sloane wants to see the proposal. He's on board with doing what needs to be done to keep the doors open, he just needs to see the details."

Kyle's heart leapt. It was a massive victory, and Wes' happiness was so contagious that it took him a few moments to process exactly what he'd said.

Sloane wanted to see the proposal. The one he and Wes were supposed to present. Together.

"You... already talked to Sloane?"

"He was trying to slip out early," Wes explained. "I caught him in the stairwell. I would've come to get you, but there wasn't any time. He already released a statement to the paper about the hospital's closure."

Kyle's head spun as he tried to process everything. Sloane wasn't going to close the hospital. Maybe. But he'd already announced it. And Wes managed to somehow secure the man's vote without presenting the data, or anything he and Kyle had planned together.

"How do you know he's not blowing smoke up your ass?" Kyle asked. "He could've said he'd take a look at it just to get you to go away."

"No." Wes shook his head in sharp defiance. "Tom can be... selfish sometimes, but he wouldn't do that."

That, too, must have been insider knowledge shared between him and Wes. In Kyle's mind, a man who told the local paper about a closure—and the layoffs that would surely follow—before telling the people who were going to lose their jobs was more than just selfish "sometimes." The man had obviously wanted to avoid conflict. He'd even tried to duck out before the shit hit the fan.

"I don't know what to say…" Kyle wished it was happy astonishment that made him speechless, but something else brewed beneath the surface.

Wes didn't trust him.

He'd known the man has issues with nurses. He just thought he'd been exempt from that list. Apparently not, because when it came down to it, Wes handled everything on his own and didn't spare a second thought about it.

He did, however, notice Kyle wasn't as overjoyed as he should be. "What's wrong? We should be celebrating. As soon as we drop off those reports, we should go somewhere. Fuck, not the bar, I guess. But somewhere."

Wes was a whirlwind of activity, and Kyle almost wanted to step out of the way and let him have it. But this was one of those moments where he had to speak up if he wanted anything more from this man than sex.

He'd avoided conflict with Rebecca, and look where that got him. He couldn't do it again.

"If you wanted to present it on your own, you could have told me," he started.

Wes' brow furrowed and he seemed genuinely confused. He was still close enough that Kyle could smell the slight scent of his soap. "Like I said, there wasn't much of a choice. Why is this an issue? We got what we wanted."

"Maybe," Kyle shot back. "If he follows through. I have no idea if he will. I don't know him like you do."

The older man finally stepped back, his expression hardening. "Why don't you say what you actually want to say here, Kyle."

What did he want to say? He searched his mind and found it full of conflicting ideas. Rationally, he knew he was overreacting, but the exclusion still hurt. When he probed deeper, he came up with an answer.

"I get why you don't trust anyone. I do. But if we're going to do this, we have to do it together."

Frustration etched its way onto Wes' face, and he opened his mouth to make what Kyle assumed was an automatic—and angry —reply. But then he stopped, searching Kyle's eyes. The scrutiny was so intense that he almost looked away, but Kyle forced himself to stay strong, even if it meant giving away things he hadn't acknowledged yet.

Letting out a breath, Wes approached again, tentatively resting his hands-on Kyle's arms. "We will. I promise. There's... no way I'd be able to do it without you."

There was a catch in the man's voice that might have annoyed him if he didn't know just who he was talking to. Trusting anyone, relying on anyone, was a monumental task for Wes. If he was saying this now, maybe it really had been a need to coordinate things quickly.

Maybe he was overthinking all of this, and letting his heart get involved before it should.

"Thank you," Kyle said with a small smile. "You said he's waiting on the reports?"

That spark returned to Wes' eyes, and the relief Kyle felt couldn't be understated. He hadn't managed to ruin things, then.

"In his office. Come on. We'll present them together."

Heart thudding in his chest, Kyle opened his locker and pulled out the folder the two of them had carefully pieced together that morning.

This was going to work. They were going to save Hidden Creek Memorial. And—despite Kyle's fears—they were going to do it together.

WES

The meeting with Tom went about as Wes expected it to go. The man was intrigued by the data and seemed excited to put it into practice, but his attention was torn by his phone, where he was likely texting with his not-so-patient wife.

Kyle caught on quickly, and they wrapped up the presentation before presenting all of the data. Tom wouldn't care about the numbers, anyway. That was why he'd hired an accountant. So long as it seemed plausible, he was happy, and he told them as much as he grabbed his things for the second time and started ushering them out the door.

They stood outside the director's office, Tom having already almost bolted for the stairs. Kyle was staring at the metaphorical dust cloud he'd left behind.

"I guess that was a little pointless, huh?" he said sheepishly, his gaze returning to Wes.

"Not pointless. It'll give him something to think about after June's appeased, and it's good information to release in the paper."

Even if the average person in Hidden Creek had no idea what all of the expenses were and what they meant, seeing hard data would likely make them feel better. It certainly did for Wes.

"Thanks. For letting me be a part of this. I know I'm not as invested in this place as you are," he said, glancing toward the railing that overlooked the hospital's main floor, "but it's obvious the community needs it."

Wes just smiled, his own gaze moving toward the place where he'd spent so much of his time and energy. This hospital was a reflection of everything he was. The good, the bad, and everything in between. The fact that Kyle saw it and appreciated it felt more significant than he was willing to admit.

"You said something about celebrating?" he asked with a smile.

"Normally I'd suggest Bottom's Up, but—"

"—the fire," Kyle finished with a frown. "Yeah. Jesus, I can't imagine losing your livelihood in one night like that." He let out a breath and tugged a hand through his hair, and Wes saw a glimpse of the empathy that made him such a good caretaker. Even though it had been a full week since the incident—and even though Kyle wasn't a Hidden Creek native—it obviously still affected him. The emotion was tucked away eventually, though, and he said, "Maybe Rocket? They sell beer there at least, right?"

"Rocket it is. Let me get my things."

THE DINER WAS BUSIER THAN WES HAD EVER SEEN IT. FINDING A parking space wasn't easy, and getting a table took about a half hour, during which time Kyle challenged him to a crane game battle. Considering the stuffed prizes stayed lodged in the machine, it was safe to say both of them lost.

When Tammy finally called them, Wes followed through the crowded restaurant, moving around tables and skirting past booths. They were brought past the counter with its high-seated, fire-engine red stools, too, and he noticed a familiar man seated at one of them, an empty stool beside him.

Garbed head to toe in black leather—or faux-leather, Wes really couldn't tell—the man was hard to miss. The kilt and combat boots also helped with the recognition, but it was made clear beyond a shadow of a doubt when the man spotted him. He smirked, giving Wes a salacious little wink.

Koby Duvall.

It'd been a while, but he still remembered the man. The definition of a free spirit, Koby had been one of the few people he'd found who was truly okay with a one-night stand. He hadn't tried to call or text afterward. He hadn't gotten annoyed when Wes kicked him out. They'd had a good time, and then they'd parted ways with only a mutual memory to link them to one another.

He wasn't worried about Koby making a scene, despite the fact that he seemed deep into his cups. He was more worried about Kyle's perception. Especially when Koby decided to verbally acknowledge him.

"Wes." It was said with a nod, and a knowing curve of his lips as he looked at Kyle—whose attention he of course had caught.

"Koby," he responded with the same nod.

That was the end of the interaction, but Kyle was grinning like the cat that ate the canary. He kept quiet as they were led to a small booth near the back, but once they were given menus, Kyle spoke.

"Friend of yours?" There was a playful light in his eyes that Wes would have found attractive if he wasn't on the receiving end of it.

"One-night stand." He wasn't going to sugarcoat it. As much as some part of him feared Kyle's reaction, this was who Wes was. He'd never made any claims to the contrary.

"He's cute," Kyle observed, glancing over at Koby again. "I mean, this is coming from a guy who thought he was straight, so take it with a grain of salt."

"We had a good time, but he never tried to make any more of things than what was there. It's in the past."

Before Kyle could respond, Tammy came to take their drink order. Those few minutes were agonizing as he watched the myriad of expressions that played on Kyle's face. Playful amusement first, then a dawning realization surpassed by obvious unease. He started fussing with the paper napkin ring as Tammy went on about the specials, and Wes almost asked her to just leave.

But she finally went away on her own, and Kyle broke the silence again.

"I'm not jealous or anything, if that's what you're worried about. Whatever this is between us, I'm not expecting some crazy commitment. I just got out of a situation like that, anyway."

He rambled on, growing more unconvincing with every word. Or maybe Wes was just projecting. He wasn't sure, but he knew he needed to set things right regardless.

"Our situation is different," he said, reaching across the table to rest his hand atop Kyle's fidgeting one. I'm not going to make any promises. I don't know if I'm even capable of doing something long term anymore."

It was a reality he hadn't admitted even to himself thus far. When Adrian died, it closed a door in Wes' heart. He had no idea if it could ever be opened again, or if he even wanted to open it.

He wasn't going to lie to Kyle and pretend like this was going to last forever when he had no clue if it would last beyond the week. But there was one thing the other man needed to understand.

"This isn't just about sex to me. It may have started off that way, but... that's not what it is now."

He wanted to say what he felt, but the words wouldn't come. He'd never been very good at expressing his feelings, after all, and Adrian had always hated sentimentality.

Wes got the impression Kyle had a gentler soul and a more tender heart, though. It shone through in the way he treated his patients, and even now as a slow smile bloomed across his features.

So in lieu of being able to express himself with words, he just took Kyle's hand in his own and squeezed it gently, gratified by the squeeze he received in return and the warmth of the younger man's smile.

"Well, now that that's sorted," a wicked grin played across Kyle's lips, "how was he?"

Wes snorted. It was obvious the man was messing with him, and he was curious how far this game of chicken could be pushed. Looking back at Kody, he said, "Not bad. I don't have a performance scale or anything, but if I hadn't been sticking to one night as a rule, I might have looked him up again."

It was the truth, but he kept a careful eye on Kyle to see how that admission went over. The other man just laughed, though, and then cringed in the most exaggerated way possible. "'Not bad?' That's how you describe somebody you'd fuck again? Just how high are your standards?"

Their drinks came soon after, temporarily suspending the game. After they placed their orders, things continued, culminating in

176

Wes rattling off several bogus criteria and Kyle chiming in with a few of his own as they shared a pizza.

Talk eventually turned more practical as they discussed the fundraising efforts for the hospital.

"We could do it at the park," Kyle suggested, "then maybe have a wrap-up here. Do you think the owner would agree to that?"

"I don't see why not. Fred's a pretty easygoing guy. In fact..." He summoned their waitress over with eye contact and a friendly smile. "Is Fred still here tonight?"

"Oh yeah, he's in the back. You need to talk to him?"

With just a bit of effort, Wes pulled some of the strings granted to him by being a lifelong member of the community and Tammy left to tell Fred to come out to their table when he had the chance. Kyle's eyes lit up, a bright smile on his face when the owner of the diner did just that about ten minutes later.

Fred was a rail-thin man in his early forties with straw blond hair and a messy beard. There were faded circles under his eyes and lines etched to his face—the marks of a man who was working harder these days. But other than that, he looked nothing like the stereotypical diner owner.

"Hey, Wes," he greeted, "if this is about the hospital, I already know. Couldn't fucking believe it when I heard."

"...Heard what?" Kyle asked, with the hesitant tone of someone who already knew the answer.

Wes did, too. It sank like a stone in his gut before Fred even confirmed it.

"The hospital's closing," he said. "Matt told me about an hour ago and I'm still in shock. I know it'll be rough on you, but what are the rest of us supposed to do if something happens? Hell, I've got heart shit going on. Am I supposed to drive an hour to get to some crowded county hospital where they're just going to send me home with a bottle of pills?"

Out of the corner of his eye, Wes saw Kyle sit back against the booth, a heavy puff of breath blown out in a rough exhale. It was a sentiment he understood all too well; something that was only reinforced as Frank kept going on, his tone gradually leaning toward panic and outrage.

The update was going to come too late.

Instead of hearing about how the hospital was struggling but had a plan to stay open, all of Hidden Creek would know by the morning that their only healthcare facility was going to close. Rumors would fly. Misinformation would spread like wildfire.

And tomorrow, he and Kyle would have to deal with the fallout.

Whatever he'd intended this date to turn into, there was no chance of it happening now. The mood was ruined, and Wes' resolve twisted as he realized they were going to have to spend the rest of their meal making plans for damage control. Pushing his plate aside, he pulled out a pen and started writing on the paper that lined the table. Within moments Kyle did the same, working with him until Rocket closed, the pair of them desperately trying to come up with an answer.

21

KYLE

*M*onday was by far the worst day Kyle had ever experienced.

The literal moment he put on his scrubs and stepped into the hospital proper, people found him in the hall and asked about the closure. Patients. Staff. Everyone. All day long.

At first, he tried to explain the addendum that had been printed in the paper that morning. After three hours of explaining that they were going to fight to keep the hospital open, over and over again, he eventually started telling people to look at the article that ran in the Horn. Late in the day, he almost considered printing out a hundred or so copies of it to hand to people before they even opened their mouths.

It was exhausting, in every sense of the word, and that wasn't even counting the constant influx of patients trying to be seen and treated before the hospital closed. It seemed like everyone in Hidden Creek had taken the day off, and solid hours were spent calming nerves, assuring people nothing was happening right away, and helping to comfort those who were most affected by the news.

He saw Wes throughout the day, though not as often as he usually did. Other doctors had been called in to make up for the influx of patients, and there was a strict rotation going on to make sure as many patients were seen as possible.

That rotation didn't apply to the nurses, of course, who were expected to keep on top of as many patients as humanly possible, to the point where the wires became crossed several times when Beth, Vivian, or one of the other nurses walked into an exam room while Kyle was already taking vitals and establishing a base-line of care.

All the while, the same questions poured in, spoken again and again by any and everyone who walked through the automated doors.

"Is it true the hospital's closing?"

"When's the last day you'll be taking patients?"

"What happens to all my files?"

"What if my insurance won't accept another hospital?"

"How could you let this happen?"

And, most frequently and heart-wrenchingly: "What am I supposed to do now?"

Sometimes it was spoken in a rage as the patient looked for someone to take their frustration out on. Usually it was said in the midst of tears, though, as people who had nowhere else to turn came to grips with the fact that they might have to go without care completely.

It was heartbreaking, and there were several moments where Kyle considered fleeing to his car, locking the doors, and just sobbing until he got everything out. The only thing keeping him from doing so was the fact that he had absolutely no time to do so. As soon as he finished with one patient, it was on to the next. And when he wasn't actively seeing someone, he was inputting patient data—while still fielding questions.

Later in the day, though, he was far too close to snapping.

A man came in, tall and built like an athlete, demanding to speak to somebody. Kyle had been the closest "somebody" there, and so he'd been on the receiving end of the man's tirade.

"You heartless fucking bastards. What are you getting out of this, huh? You all getting a nice kickback from the county or something?" His face was so red with anger Kyle thought he might burst. "Probably got a job lined up someplace else, and fuck the rest of us. I don't know how you sleep at night."

Had he not spent all day fielding similar… concerns, Kyle might have responded calmly and maturely. Instead, what came out of his mouth was:

"What part of the hospital closing because of lack of funds makes you think anyone is getting money under the table? Seriously?"

He had more on the tip of his tongue, ready and raring to go. But out of nowhere—like the cavalry suddenly appearing over the hill—Wes spared him from making a complete ass of himself.

"Hey, Travis. I know you're upset, and you have every right to be. Why don't we talk about it in the waiting room?"

Once Kyle stole a moment to himself—locked away in the bathroom—he texted Wes his thanks.

Kyle: *I'm losing it.*

Kyle: *It's like people dropped everything they were doing as soon as they heard.*

And they probably had, he realized. Wes had said the hospital meant a lot to the people of Hidden Creek. Apparently Kyle underestimated just how much.

Expecting a response in that vein, he was surprised to get something different:

Wes: *Meet me on the roof.*

It took Kyle a long moment to understand why Wes suggested it, but then it clicked. The roof was one of the few places non-staff couldn't access without knowing the layout of the building and making it all the way to the back. Nurses, doctors, and other workers tended to go up there for their smoke breaks, and Kyle had never wished he was one of those people more than today.

Pulling two key members of staff away from the hospital right now was a recipe for disaster, but if he didn't do something, he was going to break down completely. So Kyle tucked his phone away and waded through the crowds to the stairwell, taking the detour that led to the roof access.

It wasn't exactly a smooth journey. He was stopped a few times, and even got himself turned around once. But eventually he pushed in the metal handle and found himself drawing in a big gulp of Texas air. It was a hot, humid summer day, with no chance of it cooling off until nine or so, but it felt like heaven compared to inside.

He looked around, expecting to see Wes. But the only person up there with him was an older man in an orderly's tan scrubs hunched over a lighter, trying to protect the burgeoning flame from the wind as he lit up.

"You too, huh?" the man asked after taking a long drag, his tone resembling an old war veteran.

Kyle nodded with just as much gravity, moving to stand closer to the man so he could hear him better. Wes had probably gotten detained anyway, and there was no reason for him to be a stranger, even if he didn't know this man as well as he'd liked.

"Hell of a thing. Never thought I'd see the day I had to leave this place." He took another drag, blowing out a thin cloud of smoke.

Kyle had seen the man before, though he couldn't remember his name. Albert, maybe? Or Alan. Something with 'Al' in it. He wasn't as efficient as some of the other orderlies, but he was friendly, with a good sense of humor.

"You read the article in the paper today, right? We can keep the hospital from closing. As stirred up as the community is today, I know they'll pitch in."

He had to believe that, because the alternative was bleak—especially after going through all of this.

"With cuts made." The older man gave Kyle a sad smile. "Who do you think's gonna be on the chopping block first?" The man shrugged and took another puff. "I'll have been here forty-three years in September. Every decade or so, the folks doing my job get better at it. Faster. More able to multi-task. They keep me around because everybody knows me, and because I've been here almost as long as the damn hospital. But I know when it comes to deciding who stays and who goes, they aren't going to think twice about cutting an old man who can't keep up."

He turned away from Kyle, looking over the railing. The parking lot stretched out below, with the park and its lake beyond that. It would have been a relaxing view, were the lot not full of cars and the park not obscured by the smoke of a man who'd basically given up on keeping his job.

"Before you ask, retirement's gone. Cashed it out when my wife got sick, and funny thing—they don't give the money back if your loved one dies." Jesus. Guilt stabbed through Kyle's heart, knowing he had at least some part in this. "Kids are every which way across the country, and they've got their own lives to worry about. So. Guess I'll be begging for a job over at JJ's soon."

Kyle's brow furrowed, the responsibility for this near-stranger's plight weighing heavily on him. It might have been that, or maybe just his optimism, but he spoke almost immediately, and with great conviction. "There has to be another way. They can't sack someone who's worked at the hospital so long. Patients love you, and I don't care if the other orderlies are faster—you do the most thorough job, and every nurse appreciates it."

The man turned back and smiled. "It's nice of you to talk me up, but this isn't your fight. Not like you can do anything, and neither can I."

"No. I can, and I will. I'll speak to the director. I'll do everything in my power to make sure you keep your job, you have my word on that."

He had no idea what possessed him to do it. Maybe his harried nerves, or the resigned expression on the old man's face. Whatever it was, he'd apparently accepted this as his own personal mission.

Albert turned more fully to him, a spark of hope in his eyes. "You really think it'll help?"

"I do," Kyle said.

He searched Kyle's eyes and let out a breath. He ground his

cigarette into the ash tray that rested near the railing and came close to Kyle and extended his hand.

"I can't say what it means to me that you're even willing to try." Instead of going for the shake, he pulled Kyle in for a quick hug. Just a brief touch before he was on his way, heading to the roof access stairwell—the same one Wes stood near.

His arms were crossed, and there was an unreadable expression on his face. The stress of the day was obviously taking its toll, and Kyle went to him with what he hoped was a warm smile.

But Wes' expression didn't change. He looked to the stairwell, then back to Kyle. "Exactly how many people have you promised jobs to?" he asked, his tone flat; emotionless.

Kyle was taken aback, and he stood before Wes for several long, tense moments before even trying to answer. "Just him. And I promised him I would look into it—"

"That may be what you said, but that's not what he got out of it. There were tears in his eyes when he passed me, Kyle. That man is convinced you've just saved his job."

There was emotion in Wes' tone now. A cold, almost cruel emotion that reminded Kyle of those first days on the job, when Wes treated him like he was completely inept.

"And what's wrong with that? He's been here forever, Wes. He deserves to stay. I'm sure Sloane will see that."

"Sloane will see whatever's best for Sloane," he remarked with a surprising amount of bitterness, "and I'll be the one stuck holding the bill, having to go back and tell that man that no, actually he isn't staying."

Why? Dread seeped into Kyle's veins as he realized he already knew the answer to that. Sloane seemed like the kind of man who hated conflict, and he and Wes were close. He'd hand it off to HR, but might ask Wes to speak to him beforehand, because Wes...

"It's fine. I'm already the most hated person in this hospital, so what does it matter if I crush one more person?"

Words caught in Kyle's throat, caught between an apology and an argument. He didn't have the chance to voice either, though. Wes' pager went off, tearing through the heavy silence with its incessant beeping.

"Hold on a second," Kyle pleaded.

"I have to get back to work," he said, that cold, emotionless tone returning before he turned back to the stairs.

The door closed behind him, and Kyle's heart dropped with a heavy thud. This day was bad enough. Yet somehow, he knew he'd just managed to make things exponentially worse.

22

WES

$\mathcal{T}$hree days of insanity. Three days of wall to wall patient care. Three days of what seemed like every vulnerable citizen in Hidden Creek coming in to be seen before the inevitable end. Because even though news had gotten out that they were scaling back and doing everything in their power to avoid closure, people were still preparing for the worst.

And Wes didn't blame them. If he needed constant care for anything, he would have been terrified. It was too risky to depend on an entity for life-saving healthcare, especially when that entity admitted it might close and leave everyone in the lurch.

Three days of trying to assuage everyone's worries left Wes no time to deal with his own. It didn't help that he'd been avoiding Kyle, but there was a point to it beyond pettiness. Yes, he hadn't appreciated the guaranteed role as bad guy in this whole process, but he knew it was mostly stress that made him snap at Kyle the way he had. Once things calmed down, he'd explain and apologize and they could go back to the way things were.

That was the optimistic view, anyway. When Wes was feeling

more cynical, he tended to think that the influx of patients would eventually cease, only for Hidden Creek to find out it was losing its hospital after all.

It wasn't something he could think about and maintain his sanity. As it was, over the last three days he'd spent over thirty-five hours at the hospital, catching cat naps here and there in the on-call room. The same was true of the other doctors, and very likely the nurses, since even the union didn't do much to protect them, from what he'd heard.

The one thing he could say about it all was that they hadn't had any truly emergent cases. A few emergencies, yes, but no one who was unable to at least have a friend drive them. Most were capable of being triaged, with the most gruesome thing being a construction accident that happened while a work crew was cleaning debris away from Bottom's Up.

That changed Wednesday afternoon, though.

Wes was in the on-call room, trying to scarf down a sandwich in peace when the sound of sirens filtered in through the walls. The ambulance bay was a decent jog from where he was, and yet he could still hear the vehicle as it pulled in from the street.

Sighing at his very much unfinished sandwich, Wes wrapped it up, dusted the crumbs off his coat, and booked it to the hospital entrance where the paramedics were bringing someone in on a gurney.

"Sixty-seven-year-old female, history of COPD," Sheila said, her usual sunny demeanor dampened by the weight of the case. "Called 911 complaining of shortness of breath and severe nausea. We've had her on the O2 mask from the moment we started transporting her, but she lost consciousness about five minutes into the trip."

Rushing up to meet the team, Wes saw a familiar face, though far paler than he remembered it. "Mrs. Hartford."

She was the first patient he and Kyle had worked on together—the one they'd both made mistakes with. Admitting those mistakes was what brought them closer together, and Wes couldn't imagine doing this without him.

"Three is open," one of the nurses called, and the gurney was pushed in that direction with Wes lagging behind just slightly.

Under normal circumstances, he was able to keep his emotions separate from his work. It was impossible to do his job if he was constantly tripping all over himself. But stress and lack of sleep formed a powerful cocktail of anti-keep-it-together drugs, and Wes found his heart aching for the woman who still had so much life in her.

"Go find Kyle Harris," he instructed one of the EMTs, "and bring him here."

"Kyle's with another patient," the nurse who'd noted the room before—Beth, he thought—said as she started a line.

Mrs. Hartford was hooked up to the machines, and immediately her pulse ox monitor started beeping erratically. Her blood pressure was dropping, too, while her pulse was racing as her heart tried to keep her lungs from failing.

It was a war of attrition at this point. Her lungs were allowing too much CO_2 to pass through her bloodstream, and her heart needed oxygenated blood to function correctly. The state needed to be reversed and quickly, before—

"She's going into cardiac arrest," one of the other staff members in the room announced as the monitors beeped in unison.

"Bag her, push epi, and why the fuck haven't you left yet?" he growled the last at the EMT. "Go get Kyle!"

Even as he said it, he was already preparing the tubes, beating Beth to it. He tilted the patient's head back and tried to open her airway as much as possible so he could intubate, but the tube refused to cooperate.

"You aren't always gonna have your pet when you need him!" Beth exclaimed, "now move the hell over and let me help you before this patient dies, doctor."

The notion of Kyle being referred to as his pet made rage bubble just under the surface, and it permeated all of Wes' actions. He barked commands only to follow through on them himself seconds later, all while Mrs. Hartford's vitals spiraled ever downward.

"Dr. Monroe!" a familiar voice called, seeming horrified. Wes turned quickly to see Kyle standing away from the trauma.

"Get in here, I need you," he growled.

"You have Beth, and if I come in there now, I'll just be in the way."

"Then switch out!"

He was losing it. He could feel himself slipping back into that frantic, helpless state he'd been in right before Adrian died. He wasn't going to let it happen again. He just needed Kyle. No one else. He and Kyle could take care of this.

Apparently the rest of the hospital didn't agree, though, because Dr. Silverman also appeared, pulled off of whatever case she'd been working by a page. How long had she been there? The look on her face suggested it'd at least been a few minutes.

"Dr. Monroe, I think you need to sit this one out. I'll take over."

Wes refused to move, continuing to work on the woman. The other doctor put on fresh gloves and moved to relieve him, but still he didn't budge.

"Wes," Kyle said, his voice pleading. It was enough to make Wes look up, his eyes wild as they met Kyle's worried ones.

He stepped back without comment, pulling off his gloves in a snap of latex and shoving them into the biohazard bin. He moved past Kyle, very nearly bumping into him, every cell in his body wanting to crawl out of his skin.

"Wes! Hey!" Kyle called after him, and even followed as he stalked back to the on-call room. "What the fuck is wrong with you?"

The worry was still there, but when Wes whirled on him, he found annoyance, fatigue, and his same helplessness reflected in Kyle's eyes.

"What the fuck is wrong with me? Everything's going to hell, Kyle, and you weren't there. I needed you, and you weren't there."

The younger man's eyes widened and he looked around, but Wes was wholly unconcerned by their audience of staff and patients alike.

"Beth is more experienced than me. She would've—"

"No," Wes cut him off. "I trust you. I work well with you."

Anger flared in Kyle's eyes now, sudden and bright. "You're a doctor. It's your job to put your patients first, and that means working with other people. Grow the hell up, Wes, and do your damn job."

The words might as well have been a slap in the face. No. That was too mild. A stab in the gut was more appropriate, and one he deserved. It was punctuated by Kyle walking away, going back to the exam room he'd been working in, his demeanor shifting as he went to greet his patient again.

That was the mark of someone who deserved to be here. Even after so many hours, Kyle was holding it together. Wes decidedly... wasn't.

He drew in a breath through his nose and walked back to the on-call room, not looking at anyone else. Mrs. Hartford could have died under his care. She could still die now, because he'd been so stubborn.

Is that what would have happened to Adrian had he intervened? To this day, Adrian's death was one of the most crushing things he'd ever experienced, and made even more so by the fact that Wes had been excluded from the code. Would it have made a difference, though?

He thought of Adrian's rapid descent, despite the fact that he'd been propped up and talking before Wes left the hospital. He thought of the violent seizures, and the condescending nurse who'd ushered him out of the room. Twenty minutes later, the doctor came out to tell him Adrian was gone.

Would Wes honestly have been able to save him? He'd spent so much time thinking he could, and now he just didn't know.

The door closed behind him, the AC pumping into the on-call room and granting him some blissful relief from the stifling nature of the hospital. He sank into one of the chairs and pulled out his phone, more out of habit than anything else. A mindless scroll through his email revealed the usual suspects, but at the top —sent less than ten minutes ago—was a message from Tom. A message he'd CC'd to everyone else on the staff.

Hey gang,

This email is hard for me to write, and I'm sorry I couldn't do it in person. With as busy as the hospital's been, I don't want to pull anybody away from the patients. Hidden Creek still needs you.

But unfortunately, it's a need we're not going to be able to fill as well as I'd like. My accountant's been crunching numbers like crazy over the last few days, and I have some bad news:

We can save the hospital, but the proposed way isn't enough. We'll have to close to trauma completely. Emergent cases will need to go through the next closest hospital. We also need to make staff cuts. I don't have any information on that at this time, and I'm sorry for that. This is a difficult decision, and I need to give it thought.

I don't want to lose any of you. You're what make this hospital what it is. But if it's between keeping the lights on or not having a hospital in Hidden Creek at all, I hope you can agree that this is the only choice.

I'm truly sorry.

Thomas Sloane

Director of Medicine

Hidden Creek Memorial Hospital

Wes stared numbly at the screen. No trauma, which meant no real ER facilities, which meant Hidden Creek Memorial was going to turn into a glorified walk-in clinic with surgeons who sometimes deigned to visit and perform procedures upstairs.

It wasn't enough. It wasn't enough for the town or the patients or any of the people who worked at the hospital day in and day out. Everything they'd done, everything they'd sacrifice, and still it all amounted to nothing.

Wes' stomach churned with the realization, nausea hitting him hard as he remembered going back into Adrian's room and seeing his lifeless body. The same thing had happened to the hospital he loved, and there was nothing he could do about it.

Rushing to the bathroom, Wes sank down to the floor and retched up the little bit of the sandwich he'd managed to eat before his whole life was turned upside down.

23

KYLE

The email was the last nail in the coffin that encompassed three insanely bad days.

He didn't see it until several hours after it was sent, and that was only because Vivian couldn't stop talking about it when he went up to the nurse's station. He'd logged into his work email on his phone and the message completely staggered him. If he'd been standing, he wasn't sure he would have stayed that way. As it was, he stayed in his chair, just staring at the words for an embarrassingly long time until he was called by name to come check on a patient.

Hidden Creek was losing its emergency services, which accounted for a large chunk of why the hospital even existed. It wasn't just the cases brought in via ambulance, it was the people that could be triaged, too, most of whom had no insurance or very limited coverage.

The hospital was their only chance at care, and with those services gone, they'd be forced to drive for nearly an hour to get it, all without the guarantee of quality they'd come to expect from Hidden Creek Memorial.

Oh, he had no doubt the county would try to buy Sloane out regardless and turn this place into a walk-in clinic, but in his experience, those were money-making extensions of whatever hospital owned them. Many had the right to turn away patients because they didn't deal with truly emergent cases, and the vulnerable citizens of Hidden Creek would be left in the lurch.

People like Mrs. Hartford, who only had coverage through Medicare—and poor coverage, at that. She was stabilized now. Kyle's next stop was to check in on her and make sure she was getting everything she needed. But where was she supposed to go to treat complications from her COPD in the future?

It was devastating, and he was absolutely helpless to do anything about it. Of course, the first place his mind turned in its desperation was to Wes, but he was fighting his own battles.

Kyle knew what lay underneath his need to control every aspect of a frenzied procedure. He understood and even sympathized with it. But he also knew that Wes' tendencies had and would continue to endanger patients, and his lack of trust—while not extended Kyle's way just yet—could easily swing in that direction.

And that wasn't even mentioning the harsh, public thrashing Kyle had given the man. Words that needed to be said, but maybe not in front of the other nurses and medical staff.

He intended to apologize once all this was over, but he doubted it would make a difference. This seemed like the death knell as far as their burgeoning relationship was concerned. If they couldn't work together without bringing their personal feelings into it, it would be better if they just... didn't have those feelings at all.

Easier said than done, as every time he saw Wes in the hospital he felt a sharp pain deep in his chest. He wanted to go to the man, comfort him and steal him away to someplace quiet where he could make sure he rested and ate something. But knowing Wes, he could imagine the attention would be unwanted, and the patients needed them both, besides.

Case in point, he set his own personal drama aside and made his way to Mrs. Hartford's room. They've moved her upstairs, mostly because of a lack of beds on the ground floor. She would've been moved up there eventually, since she'd been formally admitted, and Kyle was glad to see that she could recover someplace far more comfortable.

Putting on his bravest, friendliest face, Kyle knocked before entering her room. He'd expected to find her resting, but she was sitting up, extra pillows propped behind her, the TV on above him.

"You must be feeling better," he said dumbly, somewhat amazed by her resilience. This was an almost seventy-year-old woman who'd gone into cardiac arrest not six hours earlier.

"And you must be exhausted. You want the bed?" she asked, patting the side of the bed.

Kyle gave her a genuine smile. "Don't you worry about me. I'll be heading home soon, I just wanted to check on you first."

"Still alive. Still can't breathe worth a damn without these little tubes," she said, pointing to the thin tubes supplying oxygen through her nose.

"It should get easier once your blood oxygenates." He moved to the side of her bed, checking her IV and her vitals, pulling down a blood pressure cuff from the wall. "In the meantime, is there anything I can get you? More pillows? Another blanket? A better cable package?"

He expected her to laugh and joke along with him, but Mrs. Hartford just looked up at him with a sad, knowing smile. As he went to slide the stethoscope under the cuff, she put a gentle hand atop his.

"You don't have to put on a brave face for me. I know everything's going to shit."

"You heard, huh?"

"Hard not to. It's all anybody around here's been talking about since I came to," she said, removing her hand so he could get the vitals he needed.

Kyle was quiet for a moment, concentrating on her pulse as he inflated the cuff by hand. The needle veered wildly, finally settling on a blood pressure that was at the low end of normal.

"There's still a chance things will work out. And you don't need to be thinking about any of that right now, anyway." The sound of Velcro filled the brief silence as he pulled the cuff off. "You need to focus on getting better."

"Honey, I am way too old to buy any of that bullshit," she said, arching one brow at him. "Unless you're some kind of saint, I know you don't believe things are just going to magically work out. Not now."

She was right, and the weight of that truth hit him hard. It felt like a sudden pressure on his chest, as though he were the one who'd experienced cardiac distress. The ache bore deep, reaching him on a level he didn't expect, in a way that wasn't just about the hospital losing so much of what Hidden Creek needed, but also about his own losses.

His father. His relationship with Brandon. Rebecca. And now Wes. Not all of them equal, but losses just the same, and the last hurt just as much as any of the others.

"No," he admitted softly, "I don't. I wish I could say differently, but... you're right. Everything's going to shit."

"Ahhh." She gave him a sympathetic smile. "Trouble with Doctor Tall, Dark, and Moody?"

Kyle let out a reflexive snort at the moniker, but it soon clicked that she apparently knew about him and Wes. Did everyone know? They hadn't exactly been subtle, but he'd tried to keep things professional at work.

"It was bound to happen, right? You don't dip your pen in the company inkwell, and all that."

"I don't know. If I had a pen to dip, I definitely would've dipped it in that inkwell," she said, her gaze faraway as though she were picturing Wes.

A blush rose in Kyle's cheeks. He wasn't about to correct her and admit that it was Wes' pen and his inkwell, not the other way around. Not yet, anyway. Not ever, now.

"Honestly? Right now I'm more worried about you and everyone else who depends on this hospital," Kyle said, settling into the chair beside her bed where he updated information on Mrs. Hartford's chart.

"Oh, I'll be just fine. Might have to eat a bit of crow and let my daughter call around to some of the assisted living places in Houston, but I was going to end up there eventually."

God, that was horrible. She said it so casually, but when Kyle looked over at her, he could see the struggle behind her eyes. It didn't take a psychology degree to know this was a fiercely independent woman, and to have to move over to a long-term care facility because the nearest hospital was gutting its services was absolutely devastating.

"Now what'd I just say?" she demanded. "You stop worrying about this right now. None of this is your fault, and you've got your own life to sort out. And other patients to tend to," she pointed out with a self-righteous nod.

There were tears glistening in her eyes, and Kyle's heart cracked just a little bit more. He wanted to stay, but it was obvious she needed to be alone right now.

"I'll go," he said softly, laying a hand on her arm. "But I'll be back a little later."

"If you must," she managed with just a hint of dramatic flair. Kyle stepped back, slotting the chart into the edge of her bed, then started reluctantly toward the door. "Oh, and I wouldn't say no to another pillow."

BY THE TIME KYLE CAME BACK LATER THAT NIGHT, ALL SIGN OF Mrs. Hartford's tears was gone. She was her regular spunky, sassy self, joking with the orderly who'd come in to change her sheets.

She was stronger than all of them, by far. Since the news broke, he'd witnessed his co-workers caring for patients while distracted, fighting back emotions at every turn, some of them even leaving before their shift ended just to get away from it all.

He didn't blame a single one of them. It was a very thin thread holding Kyle together, keeping him from doing the same. But that thread was there, and it allowed him the chance to appreciate the differences.

Daisy Hartford had grieved her lost independence, but then she'd gone right back to trying to make the people around her happy. She deserved to live life on her terms. She deserved to have a facility that could help her—save her—if she ever needed it again.

And when that became the focus of his thoughts, he was brought back to a time a couple of months ago, when he was researching the viability of rural hospitals.

He'd done it again when searching for solutions, he just hadn't been in the right frame of mind. He'd been searching for ways to cut corners and still keep the lights on.

But what if there was a way the hospital could afford its trauma designation? What if they could make themselves desirable to people from all walks of lives, for services they couldn't get anywhere else? The thought wasn't an original one. He'd found mention of it in several of the articles he'd read. But back then, he'd overlooked it.

Now, it was the only path he was willing to take forward. It had to be, because the alternative was something the people of Hidden Creek couldn't withstand. So when his shift finally ended, Kyle headed straight home and fired up his laptop. He didn't eat. He didn't sleep. He just searched for an answer.

And finally, in the early hours of the morning, when it was still pitch dark outside, he found one.

24

KYLE

*T*he problem with having an epiphany so late at night was that he had no one to help him work through it. Kyle did everything in his power to work it on his own, but he was exhausted and running out of time. He needed manpower, and asking Wes to help was out of the question right now. Instead—after wrestling with his insecurities for a good fifteen minutes—he texted the one person he knew he could rely on.

Kyle: *I really hate to ask on such late notice, but are you available?*

Brandon: *What's up?*

Rather than explain via text message, Kyle called and filled his brother in on the situation. Brandon knew about the hospital closing and then not closing, but he didn't know about the newest development or the idea Mrs. Hartford had prompted.

"So you think this will save the hospital? Actually save it?" Brandon asked.

"Honestly? I don't know, Bran. But I'm not going to just roll over and take it."

There was a pause on the line, then his brother said, "Katie's asleep. Why don't you come on over? Bring a laptop or a tablet or something and we'll sort this out."

His MacBook was still stashed in his car, so Kyle made his way almost immediately over to Brandon's, stopping to get some iced coffee for both of them first.

He reached Brandon's house around three, and the porch light was on and waiting for him, the front door unlocked. Moving as quietly as he could into the house, he greeted his brother with the intention of telling him thank you. Brandon pulled him into a tight hug instead.

"How are you? Can't imagine going through that rollercoaster," he said, drawing back.

"I'm..." Over three days, no one had asked him that. "Not great. But I'll be better if I can put together a plan."

Brandon nodded and the two of them got to work, taking up residence on his large couch. The TV played something quietly in the background—one of the shows Brandon had watched too many times to count, he explained, and something he just left on for some white noise—and the brothers scoured the internet, starting with the article Kyle found the last time he'd done this.

It took several hours and a refill on coffee that Kyle was all too happy to duck out and get, but they managed to find information on what it would take to turn Hidden Creek Memorial into a Critical Access Hospital, and how they could convert some of the beds for long-term use, hiring on the staff needed to establish a skilled nursing facility.

"So what does all of this mean, exactly?" Brandon asked as they bookmarked and printed out several pages.

"Right now Hidden Creek Memorial is designated as an Acute Care Hospital. We don't have the resources to keep patients for more than a few days, sometimes as much as a week. Emergent and triaged cases make up the bulk of our patient spread, and the people who come in for those services tend not to have great insurance, which puts the hospital at risk financially," Kyle explained. "CAH designation would allow us to keep our trauma designation while expanding our long-term care options. Some of the acute care beds would get turned into long-term care beds, and as long as we met the qualifications, we'd be reimbursed for participating in Medicare."

"Okay," Brandon said with a quiet laugh, "I'll pretend like I understand all of that. What I'm getting is this will help the hospital out financially while still letting you keep the ER open, right?"

Kyle smiled at his brother. They were both exhausted, and Brandon had nodded off several times already. "That's the gist, yeah. Instead of cutting back, we expand."

"What do we need to do to make this happen?" he asked, stifling a yawn.

"You need to go to bed. I'm going to print out some more things and brainstorm a bit more."

But Brandon shook his head, reaching for his coffee. "No. I'm in this for the long haul. Even if you weren't my brother, I can't risk something happening to Katie and then taking an hour to get her to a doctor."

Were he not so tired, Kyle might have argued more. As it was, he just nodded and filled Brandon in on the rest of his plan. They worked for another couple of hours, until the sun almost threatened to come up.

With the absence of coffee, Brandon had cranked the AC so they could both keep awake, but Kyle's limits were quickly being reached. He'd let Vivian know he needed to start his shift a bit late. After staying at the hospital for so long the past few days, there was no way he could function on another sleepless night.

But as he was getting his things together, Brandon had one last observation to share.

"I'm surprised you didn't ask Dr. Monroe for help on this."

The mention of Wes shot a pang of longing through Kyle. He missed the man. He missed how things used to be. And honestly, if he wasn't so focused on this, he would've spent all night tossing and turning, worrying about Wes.

But there was too much at stake, and Wes wasn't his to worry about anymore. Maybe he never had been.

"I'm not exactly sure Wes is into talking to me right now, even about that."

Brandon's brow furrowed, his concern obvious even through the fatigue. "What happened? I mean, you two were involved, right? And you worked really, really well together, at least where Katie was concerned. Seemed like a perfect fit to me."

It had, before all this mess, though Kyle could admit he'd had on a pretty effective pair of rose-tinted glasses.

He explained everything to Brandon, though. Wes' inability to trust anyone—including Kyle, sometimes. His own dismissal of Wes' breakdown, an admission that made his heart ache more fiercely than he anticipated. And that wasn't even mentioning the fact that some part of him wondered if Wes had just been the very different rebound from Rebecca.

Brandon listened through all of this, his features pinching more and more. He'd never been good at hiding his emotions when they were kids, and it seemed he still retained that trait into adulthood.

"Kyle, I want you to know I say this with love, but you're being an idiot."

Kyle blinked at him, caught off guard by that. He'd expected commiseration. Maybe a gentle talking to. Not a flat-out statement of his stupidity.

"I'm sorry?"

"You heard me," Brandon said. "Look, I know things are difficult right now, but if you don't fight for this, you're going to regret it."

Guilt stabbed at Kyle, his lack of familiarity with Brandon's adult life rearing its head again. "Is that what happened between you and Katie's mom?"

Brandon shook his head, a sad smile on his lips. "No. This was before I met Dani. Before Katie was born. I was with somebody I knew was my soulmate, and I let a stupid fight be the end of it." He drew in a breath, and before Kyle could even ask, he said, "but this isn't about me. This about you and Wes. Maybe I have no idea what I'm talking about, but the way you looked at him and the way he looked at you... I've seen that before. I've felt it. And I know it's worth fighting for."

Kyle swallowed the lump of emotion that suddenly rose in his throat. Emotion he'd tried so hard to suppress since everything went to hell. The hospital had to be his priority, but... what about after that?

Could he really live with himself, knowing he just threw in the towel on a future with Wes? And that wasn't even counting the fact that he was effectively making the decision for the other man, something he swore he'd never do after Rebecca did it to him.

He looked at his brother and that guilt rose again, along with a sharp sadness he hadn't expected. "Bran... you've always been amazing to me, and I know I haven't done the same for you—"

Brandon held up a hand to stop him. "Nope. Not going there." His expression softened, a smile blooming on his lips. "We were kids, Ky. You don't owe me anything. Though... actually..." His gaze moved skyward as he thought on it for a second. "Yeah, you do. Get the hell out of my house and go save the hospital. Once that's done, you talk to Wes."

Kyle could only laugh. "Okay, okay. But I need some sleep first."

"Fine. Bed, then you save the hospital. And talk to Wes." A raised brow made it clear that he was deadly serious, though the smile killed it a bit.

"I will," Kyle said, and this time, he initiated the hug, giving his brother a tight squeeze. "Thank you, Brandon. For everything."

DAWN WAS BREAKING BY THE TIME KYLE FINALLY DROVE HOME. HE showered and prepared himself for what would only be a power nap, at best. Clothes changed and Vivian called, there was only one thing left to do.

Kyle looked dubiously at his phone as it sat in its charging cradle. There was so much he wanted to say, but none of it could be said through text messages.

So he climbed into bed and grabbed his phone, composing a message that said only one of those things.

Kyle: *I have a plan to save the hospital, but I need you to trust me.*

25

WES

The text came while Wes was lying in bed, trying to decide if he should even bother going in.

Depression wasn't typically a friend of his, at least not when it came to his job. He loved what he did. He loved making an impact in peoples' lives. But that was exactly the problem. He was being denied that chance. Hidden Creek Memorial would be gutted, and eventually he'd be phased out. His inability to work well with others wouldn't be overlooked any longer, because his talents would no longer be as critical.

Or he'd leave of his own volition, unable to stomach seeing the town he loved suffer.

Kyle was right. It was something he'd come to terms with while tossing and turning throughout the night. He was too close to this, so much so that it was destroying him from the inside out. It was the same thing with Adrian, and even though he'd been forced to stand down and stay out of it, he knew there would've been nothing he could have done had he been allowed to act as a doctor on the case.

In fact, he was convinced now that he might have even made things worse, which was exactly what would happen if he approached Tom again and tried to plead the hospital's case. It made him feel helpless, and he hated that feeling more than any other in the world.

When his phone chimed, Wes ignored it at first, but worry over Mrs. Hartford and his other patients took over soon enough. It wasn't a text from the hospital, though. It was a text from Kyle.

Kyle: *I know a way to save the hospital, but I need you to trust me.*

Trust. It was something Wes didn't give easily; something that had burned him in the past. Older doctors who'd taken advantage of him when he was a medical student. Men who'd told him one thing to get in his bed, then turned around and betrayed him as soon as they had the opportunity. Nurses and doctors who'd let the man he'd loved die.

Kyle wasn't like that. He was skilled and it was obvious he took his job very seriously, putting the care of his patients first. And it was Kyle who'd made him realize that the people who'd been in that room when Adrian died had likely done the same. He wasn't there. He couldn't know for sure. But he knew if he were the one in their position, he would have done everything in his power and it still wouldn't have been enough.

Maybe he cared too deeply about Hidden Creek Memorial and his patients, but he was far from the only one who cared. Everyone at the hospital now—the people who'd toughed out three never-ending days of speculation and rumor-mongering—wouldn't be there if they didn't care.

And Kyle...

Kyle was something special. He'd sensed it from the beginning, though he'd done a fantastic job of keeping it far away from his heart. He'd just wanted another person to conquer—someone he could use and cast aside before they got too close. Before he had to trust them.

And yet he trusted Kyle far quicker than he'd trusted anyone in a very long time. It was why his attraction to the man was more than just physical. Why he'd learned to appreciate everything Kyle brought to his life, both personal and professional. And why he'd eventually handed over his heart to the man without even realizing it.

He had no idea when it happened, but it hurt to think of him now. Whatever they had was likely over, unable to survive the storm that had been kicked up by the hospital's closure. He wanted to feel bitter about that, to blame it on outside forces, but instead he just felt... empty, in a way he hadn't since Adrian died.

Another piece of his heart was missing, kept by a man who likely didn't even know it, and didn't feel the same. But somewhere along the way, he'd come to love Kyle Harris, and that was why he responded to the text.

Wes: *I trust you.*

Wes: *Let me know if I can help.*

Kyle: *Meet me in the on-call room around 5 pm.*

Putting his phone away, Wes got himself up, got showered and dressed, the smallest sense of hope coming to life inside of him. Maybe he could do something to save the hospital after all. Maybe the best thing he could do was to stay out of everyone's way.

THROUGHOUT THE DAY, HE SAW KYLE PASSING ALONG INFORMATION, a clipboard in one hand. Every now and again he handed that clipboard over, along with a pen, and whoever he was talking to wrote something—likely a signature.

By the time five rolled around, after yet another busy day, his curiosity was getting the best of him. As soon as he was able, he made his way to the on-call room and found Kyle there, already waiting.

His skin was flushed, his eyes bright with excited determination, and Wes had never seen him look more irresistible than he did in that moment. If this were just a week before, they would've been meeting here for completely different reasons.

"Thanks for coming. I know things have been crazy."

"The least I can do," Wes admitted.

That earned him a curious stare before Kyle continued, offering up a thin binder's worth of information.

"This is a detailed plan about how we can turn Hidden Creek Memorial into a Critical Access Hospital, with staff and facilities for long-term and mental health care. I know it's sudden, but I'd like your support on this."

He held up the clipboard, as well, revealing row after row of signed names.

"This is a list of all the people who've agreed to put in the work to get it off the ground, and how much we'll need to raise if we go the fundraiser route. It's going to mean some volunteer hours, and some long shifts. I don't expect you to—"

Wes held out his hand, cutting Kyle off mid-sentence. After a moment, the man handed him the clipboard, and Wes removed the pen from his coat pocket, adding his signature to the list.

"Of course I'll help. And I'll support your idea completely."

Kyle let out a long breath, a tentative, almost shy expression curving his lips. It was so tempting to pull him close and kiss him, but Wes had to maintain boundaries. If he didn't keep track of them now, it would be that much harder later.

"That's... that's really great, Wes. Thank you. I know you have history with Sloane. I'm actually going to meet with him and the hospital accountant right now..."

"Do you want me to go with you?" Wes asked cautiously.

"Only if you want to."

Was this where they were now? Stepping around each other, walking on eggshells? Kyle was likely afraid he was going to lose it again. It was a wonder he was even asking.

But he did want to go. He wanted to know how this was going to play out.

"I do," Wes said, "but only to support you."

Kyle's smile slowly grew and he nodded. There was a moment—brief, and maybe just in Wes' mind—where he sensed a note of longing behind that smile. A pang that matched the one he felt deep inside. But it was replaced by a look of determination, and soon Kyle was focused on the task at hand.

THE MEETING WITH TOM FELT DIFFERENT THAN LAST TIME. MAYBE because he'd purposefully taken himself out of the driver's seat, but Tom's "it can't be helped" nature had turned into something resembling misery over the past few days. He would've had to have been heartless not to be affected by the outcry of community and staff, and Wes knew that wasn't the case. It was a difficult position, one Tom had done for a very long time. He deserved a break, but it seemed even he realized the cost was too high.

Wes stayed quiet as Kyle presented everything he'd gathered to Tom and the hospital's accountant. He started at the beginning, explaining what CAH certification was and what it meant, and presented the many ways it would benefit Hidden Creek—and the reimbursements the hospital could expect for participating.

He also presented information from the town including the percentage of people on Medicare, the patients who said they'd make use of a skilled nursing facility—something else he'd apparently gathered throughout the day—and the list of nurses, doctors, and medical professionals who had agreed to lend their time and expertise to this program at no extra cost to the hospital.

"I'm going to have to run an analysis," the accountant said, looking over the paperwork, "but everything looks to be in order. Mercy converted five years ago, and they were able to keep their doors open. The only thing is..." He looked to Sloane then. "I can't promise this'll put you in the black. It might take years. It might never happen."

"That's where the fundraising comes in," Kyle pointed out. "It won't be a perfect stop-gap, but it'll be something."

The accountant nodded, looking over at Sloane. "What do you think, Tom?"

"I think..." He picked up the binder, flipped through it a bit, then sighed. "I think the community deserves everything we can give them. And if my wife can't understand me having to stay on for a little while longer, then she's not the woman I married."

There were still details that needed to be ironed out, and a lot of it hinged on the fundraiser, but Wes couldn't feel anything close to cynicism. The hospital was going to stay open at full capacity, and they were going to do even more to help the community. He could see it in Tom's eyes. He knew what needed to be done, and he was willing to do it.

And it was all because of Kyle.

When the two of them were dismissed so Tom could work with his accountant some more, Wes lingered in the hall just long enough to say what needed to be said.

"You saved this place, Kyle. And I… I can't really overstate how much that means to me."

Kyle smiled at him, his expression softening. That look returned again—the look that mirrored what was in Wes' own heart. He wanted to lean into it, cherish it, grab on and never let go. But as Kyle started to open his mouth, he was interrupted by several voices coming from the stairs.

"Well?"

"Did he agree?"

"Are we keeping the hospital open?"

Vivian, Beth, and Dr. Silverman crossed the distance to the two of them, all three looking cautiously optimistic.

"Nothing's set in stone yet. We have a fundraiser to put together, and it'll all depend on us getting certified, but—"

"But we've got a chance," Vivian said.

The sounds of delight when Kyle agreed with her echoed through the hospital, bringing more people up from the stairwell. And with every new person, Wes let himself drift further and further outside of the group.

They were going to save the hospital, but he was still Dr. Wesley Monroe, the man who'd made an enemy of every single employee of Hidden Creek Memorial.

This wasn't his win to celebrate. It was Kyle's. So he slipped away, stopping just long enough to talk to Al when the man flagged him down.

"I wanted to thank you, Doctor," he said, his voice thick with emotion.

That in and of itself was a surprise. Wes didn't feel like he'd done much, and he wasn't certain it made up for all the years he'd neglected the staff and blamed them for things that weren't their fault.

"You came through for us in the end," Al said, as if answering his unasked question, "and I really appreciate it. Even if this doesn't work out, I know you fought for us."

"Kyle fought for you. All I did was get out of his way," he said with a small smile, resting his hand on Al's shoulder. It was such a simple, human touch, but he realized he'd never made a conscious effort to do it before. Not with the staff who made this place what it was, at least.

Al didn't argue, thankfully, and Wes headed downstairs to do his rounds for the evening before calling it a night.

It was better this way. The more time he spent around Kyle, the more likely he was to confess his feelings. If the other man felt the same...

But no. He was too close to the situation again; just seeing what he wanted to see. He would nurture his professional relationship with Kyle and give everything he had to it. And their personal relationship would dissolve until the pain of losing it didn't ache anymore.

At least, that was the hope.

26

KYLE

*T*he hospital celebrated well into the night—as much as they were able to around treating patients, at least.

Someone's phone was docked at the nurse's station, their iTunes library blaring as medical staff and patients alike made the most of the good news. Spirits were high and soaring ever higher as the night went on, and Kyle was wrapped up in the best of it, feeling more at home than he had anywhere else in his life.

Except for the fact that something was missing. Or rather, someone. He thought he'd seen Wes at first, going about his work, moving along the outskirts of the celebration. But then he'd just disappeared, and that hole in Kyle's heart that had been carved out long before Rebecca's betrayal took keen notice.

His enjoyment faded after that, and he spent a good half hour searching for Wes, eventually making it full circle back to the nurse's station.

"You haven't seen Dr. Monroe around, have you?" he asked Vivian, who was in the middle of dancing to a Supremes song.

"Oh he left a while ago."

It hurt to think Wes had just vanished without even saying anything to him, but then... Kyle hadn't exactly made his feelings known yet. He'd focused on the hospital first, assuming Wes would be there once that was resolved. Now, because of his foolishness, he might have lost the man forever.

"You did a number on him, you know," Vivian said, still moving to the music. "If I didn't know any better, I'd think he actually sees nurses as people now."

She winked, making it clear she was joking, but Kyle's smile was tight. "I didn't do anything. Wes made his own choices."

Vivian nodded, the motion eventually moving in time to the music. She extended her hand when a patient walked up, letting them pull her into a dance.

Calling over her shoulder, she said, "Are you gonna hang around here all night, or are you going to go get your man?"

His shift was already over, and he didn't want to celebrate if he couldn't do it with Wes. There was nothing keeping him here, and everything pushing him toward the man he loved. The choice was easy, and Kyle's expression softened.

"See you tomorrow, Viv," he said, heading to his locker just long enough to get his phone, wallet, and keys before he made his way to Wes' place.

THE DRIVE WAS ONE HE REMEMBERED, AND HIS HEART POUNDED AS he pulled into the parking lot. He took the elevator up, stopping before Wes' door and gathering his courage. There was a chance Wes would reject him. Kyle had been convinced things were over between them, after all. But he wasn't going down without a fight, and he knocked on the door with a firm, steady hand.

He was still thinking of what he'd say when Wes appeared, wearing a loose, sleeveless shirt and sweatpants. He hadn't shaved the beard growth from the last few days, his hair was a mess and his clothes were rumpled from what was likely a nap, and his gray eyes took in the sight of Kyle with a mix of surprise and relief.

It was too much for him to resist and he decided not to say anything at all, instead opting for the more reckless path that better expressed why he'd come. His hands moved to the sides of Wes' neck, his thumbs brushing over the man's stubbled jaw as he drew past the threshold and kissed him, passion and heart blending as their lips met.

Wes was still for only the briefest moment before his own arms came around Kyle, pulling him flush against his body as he returned the kiss.

It was the answer Kyle had been hoping for, and he savored that kiss as long as he possibly could, reacquainting himself with the feeling of Wes' lips—soft to the touch, yet firm against his own—and the scrape of his stubble. He relished the way it felt to be in Wes' arms, the taller man fully enclosing him, his fingers curled in Kyle's scrubs.

When the need for breath became overwhelming, Kyle finally broke the kiss, pulling back just enough to look at Wes. The two traded breaths for several moments before he said, "You left without saying anything."

Wes let out a soft breath through his nose. "I didn't want to spoil the celebration."

The hand resting at Wes' neck moved up to cup his jaw. "You're part of the reason there's anything to celebrate at all," he insisted, "but that's not what I meant."

Wes searched his eyes for a long moment, the steely grey seeming to lighten as he did. "I... wasn't sure where you and I stood. I'm not exactly the easiest person to deal with, in case you hadn't noticed." His lips curved into a slight smirk. "I either close myself off completely or I get way too close. There's no in between."

If this was Wes' attempt to ward him off, it was a weak effort, and Kyle made his own position clear by kissing him again. Not as long this time, but just as sweet, the taste of Wes lingering on his lips.

"It's not a fault to be invested, Wes; to care about people the way you do. It's... one of the things I love about you," he admitted, a shy smile overtaking his confidence.

Wes' eyes widened slightly, and when the light caught them they almost looked pale blue more than the grey he'd thought them to be.

"You heard me," Kyle said softly. "I love you. I don't know if you feel the same or not, but—"

"I do," he said quickly, his expression so close to incredulous. "I do."

Wes' fingers curled more tightly against Kyle's back, drawing him even closer, their bodies pressed against one another. He swore he could feel the other man's heartbeat in that moment, and his own heart squeezed in recognition when Wes bent to kiss him.

While the last two kisses had been sweet, this one conveyed a flood of emotion that threatened to overtake Kyle. All he could do was hold on to Wes and return it, his lips and tongue meeting the other man's, the warmth of Wes' body drawing him in.

He hadn't even realized the door was still open until Wes reached behind them to close it—and then promptly backed him up against it, the breath temporarily leaving him. He followed with another kiss, this one with more intent behind it, a fact that made Kyle very aware of how closer they were.

There were times when he might have preferred a slow seduction, but right now, he needed to be as close to Wes as possible. So close that even being flush against him wasn't enough right now. His arms slid over Wes' shoulders, hands locking behind his neck as he hooked one leg over the man's hip. Wes complied easily, moving his hands to Kyle's thighs to support him, lifting him up so that his legs wrapped around Wes' waist while the taller man pinned him against the door.

They kissed until they were both breathless, pushing past the discomfort just so they didn't have to break apart. But even when their lips left one another, their mouths found other ways to stay occupied. Wes kissed along his throat and neck as his hands slid under Kyle's scrub top and over his abdomen. Kyle drew the lobe of Wes' ear into his mouth as he rolled his hips against the man, desperate to feel him.

And desperate to get out of what had become very constricting clothes.

Wes must have felt the same, because he moved his arms under Kyle's ass and lifted him up, away from the door. Kyle let out a soft, surprised yelp, then buried a laugh against Wes' neck as he was carried through the living room.

His cheeks burned, but once he recovered his dignity he took full advantage of his position, drawing Wes' bottom lip into his mouth, making the man groan and forcing him to push Kyle up against the nearest wall.

"Keep that up and we won't make it to the bedroom," he said with a growl, nipping at Kyle's jawline.

"I don't see the problem here."

Wes looked up at him, his eyes almost molten, sending a shiver racing down Kyle's spine. "As good as fucking you against this wall sounds, I don't think it's a long-term solution."

His voice was deep and thick with need, and Kyle shuddered as he unpacked all of the delicious promises in that sentence. There was no doubt in his mind they'd keep going until they just couldn't anymore, but those two words—"long term"—spoke of something that would last beyond tonight, too.

"Don't let me stop you, then," he said, some of that sass coming out.

Wes smirked and gave his ass a punishing squeeze before he returned his mouth to Kyle's and stumbled toward the bedroom. It was a wonder they even made it over to the bed, but Kyle soon felt himself being lowered with Wes following on top of him, unable to part from him.

Clothes were handled without too much thought from that point, shirts tossed aside, pants tugged down after some careful maneuvering. Kyle kicked off his shoes and was focused on getting his socks off when Wes started kissing his way down his bare torso, leaving fire in his wake.

He moaned, burying his hands in the man's messy dark hair, his hips lifting off the bed as Wes moved ever downward. There wasn't any preamble this time. In the space of a breath, Wes pulled his cock from his boxers and took him into his mouth, sucking with a frenetic energy that made Kyle's dick throb.

He threw his head back, giving in to the sensation of Wes' hot, wet mouth closing tight around his shaft. And when Wes took him deep he cried out, something inside of him tightening to an almost painful point, that frenzied, needy energy transferring freely.

Kyle's fingers curled hard in Wes' hair and he pulled the man's head up into a hard kiss. He took everything Wes gave him and then some, rolling so that their positions were switched. When the kiss broke, he struggled out of his own underwear and pulled down Wes' as well, coming back to the man to grind his naked body against Wes' before he moved downward, taking Wes' thick cock into his mouth with a confidence he hadn't possessed before.

There was no finesse in it. No teasing strokes. There couldn't be this time; they needed each other too much. Kyle simply made the most of what he'd learned from the internet, his tongue pressing against the underside of the head as he sucked. He reveled in Wes' moans and the way his thighs twitched as he tried to control himself, but there came a point where it just wasn't possible anymore.

"I need you," Wes breathed, his blunted nails digging hard into Kyle's shoulders as he urged him back up.

Their mouths met, Kyle's knees pressing into the mattress on either side of Wes' hips. Wes' hands gripped his ass, pulling him into a rhythm as Kyle ground against him, his cock slick with saliva and precum.

"Then take me," Kyle goaded, biting down on Wes' shoulder before instantly laving the spot with his tongue, earning a hiss and a shiver from the man who writhed beneath him.

One hand remained on Kyle's body, tracing a feverish caress over his ass to his back, while the other reached out behind Wes at an almost impossible angle. Kyle heard a drawer open, followed by some fumbling, and he reached out to help Wes grab the lube and condoms.

Neither of them were particularly deft. Lube got on Kyle's thighs and Wes' stomach, and one of the condoms was ripped in the process of trying to open it. Kyle could only help but laugh, catching Wes up in the joyous amusement of it all until they were both nearly breathless.

But when their eyes met again, a calm settled over him, mixing with a deep need to be connected to this man, now and always. His hands moved to frame Wes' face and he kissed him slowly, deeply, that ache returning as his heart squeezed in his chest.

Wes' hands moved between them and he slid the condom on while Kyle applied the lube, gripping his dick and making it glisten before he applied some to himself. There were no words between them, only the harsh, stuttered breathing and the beating of their hearts as their eyes met.

"Please," Kyle whispered, capturing Wes' mouth in one more kiss.

He needed this. He needed to feel this man inside him, connected to him in the most intimate sense. And as he positioned himself over Wes' cock, he soon got his wish.

Slowly he sank down as Wes lifted up, both of them in perfect sync, the same as they were at the hospital. The head of Wes' cock pressed snugly past his entrance and Kyle kept lowering himself, feeling his body stretch to accommodate the other man.

He moved in one smooth motion, not stopping until his thighs were flush with Wes'. He let out a stuttered moan, his head falling back as he gave himself over to the feeling of fullness.

But it wasn't until he lowered himself down, his elbows on the bed, hands tangled in Wes' hair, lips meeting his that he got what he wanted. Wes moved inside him slowly at first, grinding his hips against Kyle's, never breaking that connection.

When that was too much to bear, he moved faster, the rolling motion turning into powerful thrusts that Kyle met, sinking down on Wes' dick every time he thrust upward, his ass rising and falling in the air under the other man's guidance.

"Wes," he breathed, his fingers moving in a gentle caress over his lover's face.

Wes looked up at him, his eyes that same pale blue as earlier, his lips gently parted as he continued to move. "I love you," he said, arms wrapped around Kyle, cock deep inside of him.

This was what he'd needed. This connection of mind, body, and soul. It washed over him, filling him with a blissful euphoria that was almost set apart from his impending orgasm. He shuddered, driving his body down against Wes, meeting him thrust for thrust, kissing him until they couldn't maintain the breath for it anymore.

Kyle held out as long as he could, not wanting the moment to end. But eventually Wes hit just the right place inside him and his body tightened, clenching around the other man's cock as he was wracked with pleasure, his aching dick shooting between them. Wes wasted no time, thrusting deep inside Kyle and coming with a fierce shudder and a loud moan.

They lay there for a long time, chests rising and falling, hands stroking lazily over sweat-slick bodies as they caught their breath. Kyle would have been perfectly fine with the moment stretching on for an eternity, but eventually his muscles began to ache, and he knew Wes' must feel even worse.

He moved off the man, Wes taking just a brief moment to get rid of the condom before he pulled Kyle to him and held him there, against his frantically beating heart.

The night wasn't over. Not by a long shot. But Kyle lay there in the arms of the man he loved—the man he took a chance on when his heart was broken in two.

When they first met, he thought he'd just wanted something different. But what he really wanted was this. Someone who would make him feel like the only person who mattered in the world. Someone who could steal his breath away with every kiss and make him feel things he never would have imagined feeling. Someone he could let his guard down with, who let their guard down with him.

Looking into Wes' eyes, he saw the truth of it all. What they had was new, but love shone fiercely through them both. As he leaned in to kiss the man he'd given his heart, he knew with absolute certainty that they were just beginning.

EPILOGUE

WES

The fundraiser was more successful than Wes could have ever hoped.

Everyone from the hospital pitched in to organize it, with Kyle and Wes spending their off hours scrambling to get everything booked. They'd had just days to pull a plan together and it'd taken a massive, all-hands-on-deck effort to get it done. Picking a venue was easy. Kyle immediately suggested the park, and Wes was all too happy to use his charm to secure the necessary permits on such short notice. Rocket was booked for catering, with Fred promising to make the biggest pizza anyone in Hidden Creek had ever seen. A local band donated their time, agreeing to play during the slow moments, and they managed to cobble together seating and a stage—all under a canopy in the very likely event that it rained.

The auction had been Vivian's idea. Wes expected to get a few odds and ends, but from the moment they put the notice in the Horn, his cell was slammed with voice mails and texts. By the time the fundraiser rolled around, they had a wide selection of items to auction off. A Christmas wreath from Cas. A coveted spot on Rocket's menu. A twelve-month gym membership to Lift donated by Matt. Zach even offered up an all-expenses paid trip to Hawaii, something they'd decided to highlight and save for the very end.

The turnout was phenomenal. The auction was standing room only, and people wandered in and out through the afternoon to donate and share just what the hospital meant to them. As predicted, the vacation package ignited a bidding war that lasted a good ten minutes with Mrs. Hartford swooping in to snipe the last bid before it closed.

Pizza was served from a giant pie loaded down with every topping imaginable, and Wes was finally given a chance to breathe. He spent that time with Kyle and his brother Brandon while Katie played in a bouncy castle they'd rented to make sure the kids had something fun and safe to do while parents and siblings participated in the auction.

The three of them shared a picnic table, their paper plates holding slices of half-eaten pizza. Half was about all anyone could manage of the huge slices, especially in the summer heat, though the Solo cups were seeing lots of refills.

"I can't believe you guys managed to do so much in so little time," Brandon said, half-turned on the bench as he took in the scope of the event. "How much have you raised so far?"

"A little under five grand, I think. Not much, but it's a start." Kyle looked to Wes for confirmation and he nodded. "A lot of that was the Hawaii trip. Apparently Mrs. Hartford's just been looking for an excuse to spend money."

Brandon laughed. "I already saw her chatting someone up, trying to get a date for the trip."

"In the hospital just a few days ago and trying to get some action today," Kyle said with an amused smile and a shake of his head. "Doesn't surprise me at all."

"The only surprise is that she didn't already have someone in mind," Wes put in.

The whole table laughed, and Wes' attention turned to Kyle. He'd been smiling all day, and there was a warmth in his expression that drew Wes in. If this event wasn't so important for the hospital, he would have stolen the man away from the crowd already to show him how much he appreciated what Kyle had done.

"It wasn't just us," Kyle said, as if he'd somehow read Wes' mind, even though the comment was directed at Brandon. "So many people pitched in."

"He's being modest," Wes said, taking a sip of his drink. "Your brother's barely slept in the past few days."

Though admittedly that wasn't all because of the fundraiser. They'd both wanted to make the most of the time they had, and Wes had made himself a distraction on many occasions. He just couldn't get enough of Kyle.

"Well it paid off. I'm proud of you," Brandon said, reaching across the table to clap a hand on Kyle's shoulder.

Wes knew how much that meant to the man. He could see it in his eyes, and the hesitant pull to his smile. Kyle's relationship with his brother wasn't going to be repaired overnight, but they'd already made strides toward it, and the love between them was easy to see. In some ways Wes almost envied that, yet he couldn't find it in himself to be jealous. After all, so long as he played his cards right, he'd be a part of the family, too. Even if he wasn't, it made Kyle happy, and that was all that really mattered.

After a bit more chatting, Brandon chucked off his shoes and went to join his daughter and the other kids in the bouncy castle, and Wes strongly considered taking the opportunity to steal Kyle away for a few private moments before the fundraiser wrapped and the final tally was announced. Before he could give voice to all his wicked thoughts, though, a young woman approached their table.

Wes recognized her instantly, and he rose from the bench, offering a hug. "Mary. How's your father doing?"

"He has good days and bad days," she said with a small smile. "More good days than bad lately, though."

"That's great to hear," Kyle said, coming around the table to stand at Wes' side, a move that made Wes' heart squeeze in recognition.

"I know there's no miracle cure, but you two gave him something he hasn't had in a long time. Respect. It might not have seemed like a big deal to you, but it meant so much to him. And to me."

There were tears in Mary's eyes, and Wes even felt himself getting a bit more emotional than he thought he would.

"You really shouldn't thank us for that," Kyle said. "That's the way he should be treated. By everyone."

Mary nodded, swiping the tears from her eyes. "I know. And I know that's one of the things the hospital's planning to offer."

She was right. The new certification and addition of swing beds would make it possible for people like Eli to receive long-term care. It was something the community desperately needed, and Wes was looking forward to seeing it realized.

"That's why I came today. I want to make sure the expansion is the best it can be." Reaching into her purse, Mary pulled out a black leather booklet. A checkbook, from the looks of it, with a loose check inside. She held it out to Wes. "I really hope you'll accept my donation."

Wes smiled and looked down at the check, expecting a few hundred dollars—maybe a grand total. What he saw was... definitely not that.

"This is..." Kyle stammered, tripping over his words. "This is way too much, Mary."

Five hundred thousand dollars' worth of too much. Wes stared at the numbers until the zeros bled together, trying to wrap his head around what that much money would mean for the hospital. He knew it took millions to keep things operational, but five hundred thousand would do an insane amount of good.

"Put it toward helping people like my dad. That's all I ask," she said with a watery smile, still holding out the check.

Wes finally accepted it, his hand trembling as he did so. He'd hoped they might clear ten grand. Twenty if they were truly ambitious. But this blew all his previous goals out of the water in a way he hadn't expected. Looking up at Mary, he gave her a warm yet determined smile. "We will. I promise you that."

Mary gave them both a hug before she stepped away to check on her father, leaving Wes and Kyle to stare at the check in complete and utter silence. It would've been comical if it wasn't so surreal.

Kyle finally said something, wonder and excitement coloring his words. "Did she seriously just drop five hundred grand on us?"

"Seems that way," Wes said, holding out the check. He was almost afraid to touch the thing for fear of ripping it. A ridiculous thought, but he held it out as if it were the most fragile piece of paper ever made. "I'd say today was a success."

Kyle looked up at him, that excitement turning to warmth and affection and love. It shone beneath his eyes, permeating Wes' whole being, and for the moment he forgot about the insane amount of money he was technically holding. His focus turned solely to Kyle, and he knew none of this would have happened without the man. They wouldn't have made it this far to begin with. The hospital would still be closing, and Wes would still be that man who hid away from everyone.

He'd changed for the better, just like the hospital soon would. And while the hospital's success could be credited to Hidden Creek as a whole, Wes' own transformation was all Kyle.

"Thank you," he said softly, slipping his free arm around Kyle's waist and pulling him close.

"For what?"

"For not giving up on me. On us."

There were so many times he'd been difficult. So many times Kyle could have walked away. But he hadn't, and Wes knew just from looking into his eyes that he wasn't going to. Not now. Not ever.

"Sometimes it pays to be stubborn," Kyle said with a teasing grin, drawing Wes in for a kiss. "And you're worth it, Wes. We're worth it."

Over the years, Wes had let himself believe that he was too much to handle. When Sloane first announced he was closing the hospital, a part of him thought it couldn't be saved. But Kyle had proven him wrong on so many counts, and he was looking forward to being proven wrong on many more. He truly believed there wasn't anything they couldn't handle—so long as they faced it together.

ALSO IN HIDDEN CREEK

Welcome to Hidden Creek, Texas, where the heart knows what it wants, and where true love lives happily ever after. Every Men of Hidden Creek novel can be read on its own, but keep an eye out for familiar faces around town!

Don't miss a new season of Hidden Creek! To keep up to date with new releases, make sure you join us in our Facebook group here: www.facebook.com/groups/MenOfHiddenCreek/

SEASON TWO

ASHES by HJ Welch

ALLURE by Blake Roland

ACHE by Alison Hendricks

ALWAYS by Dillon Hunter

ALLIED by Max Hawthorn

ADORE by E. Davies

SEASON ONE

SHELTER by E. Davies

STORM by HJ Welch

STAY by Avery Ford

SHIELD by Max Hawthorn

SCORE by A. E. Wasp

SERVE by Ian O. Lewis

ABOUT THE AUTHOR

Alison Hendricks is devoted to creating contemporary M/M romances that are sexy and emotionally satisfying. She loves making her boys work for their Happily Ever After and believes love stories are better with just a little angst thrown in.

Born and raised in Florida, Alison has always had a passion for writing, and romance novels of all kinds are her number one escape when life gets a little too hectic.

Newsletter: http://eepurl.com/bNr7vX

f facebook.com/alisonhendricksauthor

ALSO BY ALISON HENDRICKS

FINAL STRETCH (GLEN SPRINGS #1)

Superstar NFL running back Travis Morrison has been chasing down the same dream since he was a kid. The down-home, aw-shucks, former Eastshore favorite has always known his talents lay with football, and he's never hoped for much more. But when the man he was going to marry leaks a sex tape of the two of them, Travis' golden boy image—and his world—is turned upside down in an instant. Keeping a low profile at his brother's place in Kentucky to save his career seems doable... if he can resist the temptation of his brother's smart-mouthed best friend.

Shane McMillan was on the inside track to the Kentucky Derby when a devastating accident destroyed his career and his confidence. After five years, he finally feels like he's managed to escape the limelight thanks to his best friend and the welcoming folks of Glen Springs. The peaceful life he's built rehabbing horses on his small ranch is everything he needs, until temptation arrives in the form of a disarming smile and a hot, athletic body. His best friend's brother is definitely trouble—but he's the kind Shane just can't seem to resist.

When a misunderstanding leads Travis to work at Shane's ranch, the growing attraction between them starts to burn out of control. Long, hot days lead to even hotter nights when fantasies become reality. Just as their desire starts to turn into something deeper, a photo of them becomes hot news that threatens to shatter everything they've worked so hard to achieve. With Shane's past exposed and Travis' career in jeopardy it all comes down to the final stretch.

Made in the USA
Columbia, SC
08 February 2019